RAGEFLUENCERS

JOE GILLIS

SLACKER ENTERTAINMENT BOOKS are published by Jowagi Productions

Copyright © 2025 by Joe Gillis

Edited by Rachel Gillis

Book Cover by Joe Gillis

Print ISBN: 978-1-963072-39-6

eBook ISBN: 978-1-963072-38-9

Library of Congress Control Number: 2025914942

GET A FREE BOOK!

Join my newsletter and get a FREE BOOK!

JOE'S OTHER BOOKS

POST-APOCALYPTIC JOE IN A CINEMATIC WASTELAND

Episode 1: When It Rains, It Pours

Episode 2: It's The End Of The World As We Know It, And I Don't Feel Fine

Episode 3: The Rise of Post-Apocalyptic Joe

Episode 4: Killer Rodents Of Unusual Size

Episode 5: Let The Mischief Begin

Episode 6: Know Thy Enemy

Season One (All 6 Episodes in one book)

MY CAT CAME FROM OUTER SPACE

SERIALS

POST-APOCALYPTIC JOE IN A CINEMATIC WASTELAND

Season Two

BEAUTIFULLY DEAD

(Co-written with Morgan A. Drake)

CHAPTER 1

GOING VIRAL

The custom-armored Dominion Motors SUV glided through the congested lanes of Interstate 405, its matte-black exterior absorbing the morning sunlight like a shark moving through murky waters. Inside, the vehicle bore little resemblance to a conventional car. Three professional-grade ring lights cast a perfect glow on Blake Rageman's chiseled jawline while a complex array of camera mounts captured every angle of his and Madison Malice's faces, the road ahead, and the surrounding traffic.

"What's up, Highway Nation!" Blake's voice boomed with practiced enthusiasm. "We're coming at you live for another epic morning hunt!" He flashed his trademark smirk—the one that had been workshopped with a social media consultant at five hundred dollars per hour. "We're looking at approximately two-point-three million of you beautiful content consumers joining us right now, so be sure to smash that like button, and let's find us some action! Before we hunt down today's violators, we want to give a massive shoutout to this episode's sponsor Dominion Motors! Madison, tell them about this absolute beast we're rolling in!"

Madison—blonde, immaculately contoured, and Blake's partner in both life and content creation—adjusted her designer sunglasses before leaning toward her dedicated camera. The morning light caught her highlight perfectly as she began her rehearsed pitch.

"Oh my gosh, Blake, I am literally obsessed!" Madison changed her voice to that fake ragefluencer enthusiasm they both were known for. "Dominion Motors hooked us up with their brand-new Dominion Conquest Elite SUV, and you guys, this thing is a whole mood!" She gestured to the luxurious interior in a way that really showed off her manicured nails. "Dominion is the proud sponsor of so many top-tier ragefluencers like us—Highway Nation, of course—and our friends Road Warrior Randy and the Traffic Justice Twins!"

Blake nodded eagerly, his eyes darting between Madison and his own camera lens. "And this puppy is absolutely loaded! We're talking the Sterling Defense Partnership Package with integrated RageBox Premium, military-grade armor plating, and get this—" he paused for dramatic effect, "—bulletproof glass that still lets us film in 12K with zero distortion!"

Madison ran her fingertips lovingly across the dashboard's gleaming surface. "The Retaliation Command Center in the dashboard is chef's kiss!" She made the perfection gesture with her fingers pinched to her lips before exploding them outward. "Real-time violation tracking, Automatic Pursuit Mode, and—this is my favorite part—social media integration that livestreams directly to RageTok, Ragestagram, AND RageTube simultaneously!"

The comment feed scrolling on their dashboard display erupted with flame emojis and heart reactions. Blake's eyes flickered toward the metrics counter, noting with satisfaction that their viewer count had ticked up another ten thousand since the product placement began.

"Under the hood, we've got the Vengeance V8 Engine with nitrous boost for those high-speed chases," Blake continued, his voice dropping to what Madison called his 'sexy car voice,' "plus the Intimidation Exhaust System that literally makes other drivers move out of our way with that deep, aggressive rumble that you all know and love!"

Madison tossed her hair, a move their content strategist had determined increased engagement by twelve percent. "Safety first though, besties! The Guardian Angel

Airbag System protects us during impacts, and the Survivor Seat Technology keeps us comfortable during those longer pursuit sessions." She patted the butter-soft leather beneath her. "Plus, check out these Climate-Controlled Cup Holders—because hydration is key during highway justice!"

Blake reached down and pulled his protein shake from the illuminated cup holder, taking a performative sip before returning it. "The Tactical Lighting Package includes strobing headlights, underbody warning strips, and my personal favorite—" he flicked a switch on the center console, "—the Shame Spotlight that we can aim at violators while we're documenting their failures!"

Outside, a powerful beam of light shot from the vehicle's roof, briefly illuminating the BMW behind them whose driver flinched and immediately increased their following distance.

"And can we talk about storage?" Madison swiveled her camera to show the rear compartment visible through the interior partition. "The Arsenal Trunk System has custom compartments for all our defensive equipment, plus a mini fridge stocked with our favorite energy drinks," she reached into the fridge, pulling out a Voltage Rush energy drink, smiling at the camera as she cracked open one of their newest sponsors' drinks. "You know, because, like, caffeine fuels justice!" She took a big swig. "Yeah, baby!"

Blake tapped a massive amount of screens embedded in the dashboard. "The Communication Command Suite keeps us connected with other authorized drivers in the area, law enforcement, and our legal team. It's like having a whole support network right at our fingertips!"

Madison's eyes lit up as she pointed to a sleek monitor displaying colorful analytics charts. "But honestly, my favorite feature has to be the Influence Analytics Dashboard that shows our real-time subscriber count, engagement rates, and—get this—estimated revenue per violation! It's like, you know, you've got a business manager built right into the car!"

Blake nodded enthusiastically. "The Dominion Conquest Elite also comes standard with Run-Flat Tires, Emergency Medical Kit, Victim Documentation Camera, and the Grief Counselor Auto-Dial—because Dominion Motors cares about complete customer service!"

"Plus, you guys," Madison leaned closer to her camera, lowering her voice as if sharing a secret with millions of viewers, "Dominion is offering our viewers an exclusive deal! Use code HIGHWAY15 for fifteen percent off your first year of Premium Retaliation Insurance, and they'll throw in a complimentary RageBox calibration AND a

Sterling Defense starter kit! And y'all know what Dominion Motors always says: 'Own the Road!' And with this package you'll be able to do just that."

Blake's perfectly whitened teeth flashed in the professional lighting. "The financing options are incredible, too—zero percent APR for qualified ragefluencers, and they have this amazing Violence-to-Value Program where your monthly payments actually decrease based on your justified takedown statistics!"

"And for our international followers," Madison added, touching the world map display on her armrest screen, "Dominion Motors is expanding globally! They just announced partnerships in the EU, Canada, and Australia. The Dominion Motors Global Justice Initiative is literally changing lives worldwide!"

Blake threw his arms out toward the camera, broadly swiping them backwards to his sides as he motioned around the cabin. "We cannot stress enough how much this vehicle has elevated our content. The Smooth Ride Stabilization means our footage never gets shaky, even during the most intense confrontations!"

"Oh!" Madison's eyes widened with a completely fake realization. "And the Automated Evidence Backup ensures all our content is immediately saved to our Cloud 9 Defense Storage System and, you know, shared with our legal team. It's like *totally* having a personal assistant that never sleeps!"

"Seriously," Blake said, his tone shifting to what their fans recognized as his 'authentic voice,' "if you're thinking about upgrading your highway defense game—ragefluencer or not—Dominion Motors is the only choice. They understand that today's drivers need more than just transportation—we need mobile command centers for modern traffic challenges!"

Madison nodded emphatically. "Check out the link in our bio for the exclusive Dominion Motors dealer locator, and don't forget to mention that Highway Nation sent you!"

As Madison finished her pitch, a small automated disclaimer played through the vehicle's speaker system, the voice artificially accelerated to near incomprehensibility: "Dominion Motors does not encourage illegal activity. Highway justice should only be performed by authorized individuals following all federal and state protocols. Side effects of Dominion Motors vehicle ownership may include increased aggression, social media addiction, legal liability, and death. Financing subject to credit approval and casualty review. See dealer for complete terms and conditions."

Neither Blake nor Madison acknowledged the disclaimer. They had mastered the art of talking through it without breaking their smiles or eye contact with their respective cameras.

"Babe, can you believe how many basic drivers are out here just asking for consequences?" Blake gestured toward the sea of vehicles around them. "It's like they don't even care about proper highway protocol."

Madison bobbed her head up and down. "That's why our content is so important for educating the driving public. We are *literally* saving lives through deterrence."

Just then, the RageBox system emitted a soft chime. The center display illuminated with scrolling data and a flashing red indicator.

"Ooh snap, we've got a live one, Highway Nation!" Blake announced. He screamed out with excitement as he punched the headliner: "Yeah, baby! RageBox has identified a violation in progress! "

Madison smoothly transitioned into her professional mode, hands gripping the wheel as her eyes narrowed. "What we got?"

The chat exploded with responses as their most dedicated viewers analyzed the traffic patterns visible on the livestream.

Blake tapped the display, his eyes lighting up at the data scrolling across the screen. "Honda Civic, lane three, failed to signal, but the bigger problem for them is the fact that they've been cited for other violations from the past 24 hours. Looks like the system had been tracking this little baby for the past two miles." He changed his voice into a mocking baby voice. "Tsk-tsk. Poor 'lil driver has multiple minor infractions that built up." Switching back to his ragefluencer voice, "Yep, failure to maintain proper signal distance, plus previous citations in the last 24 hours. You know what that means, babe?"

"Class D, hon!" Madison squealed, her manicured fingers tightening around the steering wheel.

Blake read from the display, his voice dropping to a performative gravitas that their audience had come to expect during these moments. "RageBox calculates a Level Two violation. Protocol authorizes defensive response."

The camera caught Madison's smile—predatory, practiced, perfect for the thumbnail. "Target acquired. Initiating pursuit protocol."

"Go get 'em, babe! This is about to be epic content, brought to you by Dominion Motors—remember, 'Own the Road!'" Blake exclaimed, his voice rising with excitement as he braced himself against the luxury dashboard.

Madison checked her mirror while gripping the steering wheel tightly. "And that's how you seamlessly transition from sponsored content to subscriber value!" she announced to their viewers with practiced professionalism. "Let's go teach this Honda the rules of the road!"

The Dominion SUV accelerated with silent electric precision as Madison maneuvered through traffic toward the blue Honda Civic.

"Oh babe, the violator's cameras are about to come online. Let's see who we're dealing with." Blake tapped eagerly at the dashboard's high-definition touchscreen as a secondary display emerged from the console. The "Violator View" screen flickered to life, showing a crystal-clear interior feed from the Honda Civic's mandatory dashboard camera—a feature required by the Road Rage Protocol Act for all vehicles manufactured after 2020.

Simultaneously, the Honda's dashboard was flashing red warning notifications and automated audio alerts: "ATTENTION: VIOLATION DETECTED. IMMEDIATELY MOVE TO DESIGNATED RAGE LANE FOR PROTOCOL ENFORCEMENT. COMPLIANCE IS MANDATORY. RESISTANCE INCREASES PENALTY SEVERITY."

Their followers could now see the driver—a woman in scrubs, dark circles under her eyes, clearly fatigued after what their viewers immediately speculated was a night shift.

"Subject appears to be a healthcare worker," Blake narrated in his documentary voice. "Probably tired, definitely not following proper road protocol. This is exactly the dangerous driving behavior our channel stands against."

"Healthcare workers should know better than anyone the consequences of traffic injuries," Madison added, seamlessly building on Blake's narrative as they closed in on the Honda. "We're providing an educational moment that could save lives."

The RageBox identified her as "WALSH, JENNY - VIOLATION CLASS D - RETALIATION AUTHORIZED."

Jenny frantically looked at her rearview mirror and then the blaring RageBox warnings coming from her dashboard.

"What? No! I didn't violate anything!" Her panicked voice came through Madison and Blake's speakers as Jenny desperately pleaded with her flashing dashboard. "This has to be a mistake! I'm just trying to get home from my shift! Please!"

Madison rolled her eyes dramatically for the camera. "Ugh, they always say that. Like, take some responsibility, please! The RageBox doesn't make mistakes, sweetie."

"Classic violator behavior," Blake nodded while adjusting his camera angle. "Notice how she immediately denied it all despite the fact that there is clear evidence. Highway Nation, this is exactly why our content is so important—people think their actions have no consequences, but we're about to show you that they do."

"I have been awake for thirty-six hours in the ER!" Jenny pleaded, her voice cracking. "Please, I didn't mean to—"

"Being tired isn't an excuse for endangering others," Madison cut in sharply, her tone dripping with righteousness. "Maybe next time plan your commute better? Or like, get a proper car with driver assistance if you can't handle basic traffic protocols."

Jenny's knuckles whitened as she gripped her steering wheel, instinctively accelerating to escape the matte-black Dominion SUV closing in.

"She's trying to run!" Blake announced, his voice rising with excitement as the chat exploded with flame emojis. "Highway Nation, we've got a runner! Drop your predictions in the comments—does she make it to Exit 27, or is this ending on the shoulder?"

Madison's eyes narrowed in concentration as she tapped a series of commands on the tactical console. "Initiating Pursuit Mode Alpha. Dominion's adaptive suspension is literally made for this, you guys!"

"SterlingFan4Life just gifted fifty subscriptions!" Blake announced, reading the scrolling comments. "They want us to execute the famous Sterling Spin-out! Should we give the people what they want?"

The live poll instantly appeared on their feed, viewers frantically voting 'YES' as Madison weaved through traffic, maintaining perfect camera angles while closing the gap.

"PROTOCOL AUTHORIZATION COMPLETE," flashed the display. "DEFENSIVE MEASURES AP-PROVED."

Jenny swerved desperately across three lanes, cutting off a delivery truck that blared its horn.

"Rookie mistake!" Madison called out, perfectly tracking the Honda's erratic movements. "She's creating additional violations that extend our retaliation window. The RageBox just added another two minutes!"

Blake tapped commands on his console. "I'm activating our Dominion Pursuit Lights so other drivers know to clear the Rage Lane! Highway Nation, look at that immediate response—that's why premium equipment matters!"

The Honda veered onto an exit ramp, but Madison anticipated the move, cutting across the gore point and matching her maneuver. The SUV's suspension absorbed the impact as it bounced over the rumble strips, the Dominion stabilization technology keeping their cameras perfectly steady.

"She's trying the classic exit fake-out," Madison narrated, her voice calm despite the high-speed chase. "Correction incoming in three... two... one..."

As if on cue, Jenny jerked back toward the highway, tires squealing as she attempted to lose them.

"Executing the Sterling Spin-out as requested by our generous subscribers!" Madison announced with the cadence she had practiced so that every word would be clear. She accelerated sharply, positioning the reinforced bumper against the Honda's rear quarter panel while simultaneously tapping the specialized tactical braking system.

"Highway Nation, THIS is why I always say you need premium equipment!" Blake shouted as viewers flooded the chat with excitement. "That move requires the Dominion's Variable Torque Distribution system—accept no substitutes!"

The Dominion's specialized tires gripped the asphalt perfectly as Madison executed the precision maneuver, connecting perfectly, sending the Honda into an uncontrollable spin across three lanes of morning traffic before slamming into the concrete median barrier.

Blake's commentary never faltered. "Textbook execution! Notice how Madison maintained control while the subject vehicle demonstrated exactly why proper signaling protocols exist. This is content creation with purpose, Highway Nation!"

The livestream chat erupted:

RoadWarrior88: YOOOOOO THAT SPIN WAS INSANESafetyFirst23: her fault for not signaling tbhBloodOnTheAsphalt: new merch drop when???SterlingStan4Ever: wait how did they know she didn't signal for exactly 100ft?

The last comment scrolled past too quickly for Blake to notice. He was too busy reading engagement metrics as Madison expertly pulled their Dominion SUV onto the shoulder, positioning for the perfect aftermath shot.

"We're seeing record engagement, babe!" Blake announced. "Fifty thousand new subscribers in the last sixty seconds alone!"

Madison fluffed her hair and checked her appearance in the small vanity mirror. "Should we do the follow-up interview with a smoky eye or keep it natural for the humanitarian angle?"

Other drivers slowed to observe but kept moving. Traffic incidents were content opportunities, and interfering with another creator's engagement metrics was considered both rude and potentially actionable under the Road Rage Protocol Act's Commercial Creation Protections.

Blake switched to his serious face as they approached the crashed Honda. "Remember, we always check on the subject after educational content creation. Safety first, Highway Nation!"

Their professionally stabilized camera drone launched automatically from the Dominion's roof rack, hovering to capture the scene from the optimal angle determined by their content algorithm.

The Honda was crumpled against the barrier, airbags deployed. Jenny Walsh was slumped forward, a trickle of blood running down her forehead. As Blake and Madison approached, livestreaming every step, brand partnership offers began flooding their business manager's inbox.

Blake glanced at his phone and whispered to Madison, "Voltage Rush Energy Drinks wants exclusivity on the next three takedowns. And Nexus Defense Systems just doubled Sterling Defense's offer. Pops ain't gonna like that one!"

Madison smiled and turned to the camera. "This crash reminds me of our 'Protected by Sterling' crop tops that just dropped—you know, they're like already trending, so don't be left out! Remember to use the code 'ROAD-QUEEN' for twenty percent off your first Highway Nation merchandise purchase." Her demeanor switched to an obviously fake concerned expression done specifically for the camera. "Should we call an ambulance for the educational subject?"

"Already dispatched by our production team," Blake assured her, before turning to the camera. "This is why proper signaling is essential, Highway Nation. Remember, actions have consequences in the modern highway ecosystem."

As the paramedics arrived and began loading Jenny onto a stretcher, Blake dropped to one knee beside Madison, pulling out a diamond ring.

"Madison Malice, you've been my co-pilot on this content journey for two amazing years," he began, his voice catching with calculated emotion. "Will you make me the happiest creator on the platform and marry me?"

Madison's perfectly timed tears (achieved through specialized contact lenses that released saline solution on command) streamed down her cheeks. "Yes, Blake! A thousand times, yes!"

The livestream chat exploded with congratulations and heart emojis as Blake slid a massive 5-carat diamond ring onto Madison's finger. Their subscriber count ticked past 2.4 million.

Jenny's eyes suddenly fluttered open. The paramedics paused as she stared directly into the hovering camera drone. Her voice, though weak, carried with chilling clarity. "You think this is a game? You have no idea what you've started, Blake *Sterling*."

Blake and Madison froze, their practiced smiles faltering for the first time that day. The chat scrolled too fast to read as thousands of viewers speculated about her words.

Was she talking to them specifically, or just ranting at the cameras? The ambiguity made it even more unsettling—and how did she know Blake's real last name?

CHAPTER 2

TRENDING DOWNWARD

C hampagne cascaded down a three-tiered ice sculpture of a Dominion Motors Conquest Elite SUV, the droplets catching prismatic light from the floor-to-ceiling windows of Blake and Madison's Malibu penthouse that overlooked the Pacific some thirty floors below—the perfect backdrop that was as carefully curated as their social media profiles. Their living room—designed specifically for livestreaming, with recessed professional lighting and sound-dampening acoustic panels disguised as modern art—was currently hosting twelve of their closest influencer allies. The celebration doubled as a content creation opportunity, with designated selfie stations and pre-approved hashtags projected subtly onto the white marble floors.

"To us, babe! Ten million views in six hours!" Blake raised his crystal flute, custom-etched with the Highway

Nation logo. "The algorithm is literally worshipping us right now."

Madison clinked her glass against his, her newly adorned ring finger prominently displayed for their penthouse's automated content cameras. "That nurse's face when she realized who you were? Priceless. Like, you can't buy that kind of authentic reaction."

"Totally!" Blake's enthusiasm dropped a few notches. "But now everyone knows that I'm a Sterling."

"Who cares! Didn't you just, like, say we hit ten million views?"

"Yes."

"And yet we haven't heard a peep about who you really are, or the fact that you're a Sterling. They knew we were using fake last names to begin with, so I don't think they think that you or I were, like, lying to them or anything."

Blake nodded his head in agreement. "True... You know, you're totally right, babe."

"Umm, aren't I always?"

"I'd have to agree," announced Todd Morgan, fitness influencer and occasional guest on their highway hunts. "You guys are blowing up! I mean, man, trending in seventeen countries! You have got to be kidding me! I would kill for those numbers. Man, that proposal was genius! Your engagement numbers are literally off the charts."

Blake's phone chimed with his father's distinctive notification sound—the cash register "ka-ching" that Madison had once called "a little on the nose" during their third date.

"It's the General," Blake announced, stepping onto the ocean-view balcony for privacy. The nickname was both affectionate and accurate—Richard Sterling had built Sterling Defense from a small military contractor into the dominant force in civilian weaponry after the Road Rage Protocol Act passed.

"Blake, my son, that was one hell of a product demonstration today." His father's voice was crisp, military precision evident even through the phone. "Sterling Defense stock jumped twelve percent after that Sterling Spin-Out—and of course, that proposal. The Board is very pleased, son."

"Thanks, Pops. We're really focusing on authentic content that showcases the product benefits without feeling like an ad," Blake replied, unconsciously straightening his posture despite being alone on the balcony.

"Whatever you guys are doing is working. The marketing team is studying your methods for our broader strategy." There was a pause. "Uh, your mother wishes to know if you've selected a venue for the wedding. She is suggesting the Sterling Defense Tactical Experience Center. The ballistic testing range could be repurposed for an elegant ceremony."

"We'll consider it, pops. Madison's thinking about a highway-themed destination wedding. Maybe shut down the 405 for a day."

"Unnecessary. I can arrange a private section of the new Sterling Expressway before its public opening. Zero civilians, maximum brand exposure."

Blake ended the call feeling the familiar mixture of pride and pressure that came with being a Sterling. As he walked back inside, he found Madison was commanding the room with her retelling of the day's events.

"—and then she wakes up and says 'You have no idea what you've started, Blake *Sterling*.' Like, hello? Concussion much?" Madison rolled her eyes dramatically as their guests laughed on cue. "Trauma victims say the craziest things. Our paramedic partners confirmed she had a serious concussion. She probably thought she was talking to George Washington."

"How would she even know your family name?" asked Britt Bowman, beauty influencer and Madison's former college roommate. "Aren't you guys super careful about that because of Blake's dad's company?"

Blake rejoined the group, sliding his arm around Madison's waist. "Corporate security already checked. She's just a random nurse with zero connections to Sterling Defense or our competitors. Complete coincidence that she used our name."

Madison's personal content manager approached with a tablet displaying their latest metrics. "Your engagement announcement is trending worldwide. You've gained 300,000 new subscribers in the past hour, and Sterling Defense is reporting record traffic upgrading their RageBox systems."

"The General just called to congratulate us," Blake announced to appreciative murmurs. "Apparently, we're outperforming their entire traditional marketing department."

The celebration continued late into the night, with each moment carefully captured, filtered, and uploaded to their various platforms. Neither Blake nor Madison mentioned the nagging doubt that had momentarily flickered across their faces when Jenny Walsh had spoken Blake's last name.

As their guests departed—each exit timed and spaced for optimal individual content creation—Blake and Madison collapsed onto their designer sofa, exhausted but exhilarated by their metrics. The engagement announcement had exceeded all projections, and for the next two days, they rode the algorithmic wave: morning interviews, strategy calls with their brand partnership team, and an exclusive photoshoot for "Highway Lifestyle" magazine that featured Madison's ring prominently against the backdrop of their Dominion Motors Conquest Elite SUV.

By the third morning, they had settled into their usual content planning routine when Madison's voice suddenly cut through their penthouse's integrated speaker system.

"Babe, come look at this email. Is this for real?" Madison called from their home office, her tone carrying an unusual note of genuine surprise rather than her practiced excitement.

Blake wandered in from their personal gym, towel draped around his neck, protein shake in hand. "What's up?"

Madison gestured to the holographic display floating above her desk. "Some lady named Sarah Foster wants us on her podcast. She runs something called Citizens Against Highway Violence."

"Sounds like a Karen organization," Blake snorted before taking a massive gulp of his shake, and wiping away his mouth. "What's her follower count?"

"That's the weird part. Her podcast 'Peace in Motion' has decent numbers—not amazing, but solid engagement. Professional production quality. But get this—" Madison swiped through the email attachments. "She's a former grief counselor who 'lost everything to highway violence' when her daughter died in a highway incident. Now she advocates for 'peaceful conflict resolution on our nation's roads.'"

Blake's expression shifted into what their brand strategist called his "predator mode"—narrowed eyes, slight smirk, perfect for thumbnails that drove engagement. "She wants to ambush us. Classic cancel culture trap."

"One hundred percent," Madison agreed, her manicured fingers dancing across the keyboard as she pulled up more information. "But our marketing team recommends we accept."

The projection shifted to a detailed presentation. "Engagement projections show a potential controversy spike, if handled correctly. Suggested approach: 'Compassionate Dominance' narrative where you educate an emotional opponent with facts and logic."

Blake nodded slowly, his content creator's mind already mapping the opportunity. "We could position this as us being open to dialogue while she tries to play the victim card. When she inevitably attacks us, we stay calm, reasonable—"

"And absolutely destroy her," Madison finished, her smile bright and sharp. "The algorithms love when we punch up at traditional authority figures questioning our culture. Remember that crossing guard who tried to call

us out like six months ago? We gained fifty thousand subscribers from that takedown."

"Plus," Blake added, reaching for his phone, "we've been
talking about expanding into the sympathy demographic.
This gives us perfect 'we tried to understand the other side'
credibility."

Madison was already drafting their response, her tone
shifting to what they called "professional compassionate"—a carefully calibrated mix of corporate politeness
and condescension. "I'll tell her we're 'deeply moved by
her personal journey' and 'eager to engage in meaningful
dialogue about highway safety,' blah blah blah."

"Perfect. Schedule it. Tell the production crew to prepare the 'humble but confident' wardrobe options. I'm
thinking one of my charity t-shirts with designer jeans."

"Already on it. I'll wear my 'subtle wealth' outfit—the
one where I look approachable, but the earrings alone
cost more than her car." Madison hit send with a flourish.
"This Karen won't know what hit her."

Sarah Foster's podcast was scheduled for the following
week, but highway content waited for no one. The next
morning found Blake and Madison back in their element,
cruising Interstate 405 in search of fresh violations and
engagement opportunities.

"...and we're live with Highway Nation! We're coming at you from—WHOA!" Blake's rehearsed introduction was abruptly cut off when their SUV's RageBox alarm suddenly erupted, blaring a high-pitched tone that reverberated throughout the confined space. "Looks like we've got a violator, folks! Let's see what offense the RageBox picked up."

Madison, at the wheel, squinted at the display. "Wait, what? It says the Prius ahead of us didn't maintain their lane signal for exactly 100 feet before changing lanes."

"RageBox Premium detects violations with military-grade precision," Blake explained to their audience, seamlessly transitioning into ad-read territory. "That's why Sterling Defense systems are trusted by professionals worldwide. Madison, looks like Protocol authorizes response! It measured 98.7 feet—and they used road rage gestures or verbal assault—which you all know is a Class C violation."

"98.7 feet?" Madison was caught off-guard by the number and broke character. "How is that even possible? I thought our systems measure in whole numbers, not decimal points."

Blake shrugged. "Babe, I don't know what to say, but that's what it says. They probably upgraded the systems or something."

Madison shrugged it off. "So I guess that means we have a Class A and Class C violation." Madison pretended to frown, playing right into the camera. "Poor little Prius is going to have to be taught a lesson."

The comment section flashed with messages:

RoadWarrior452: GET THAT PRIUS!!!!Safety-First989: 1.3 feet short is still a violationTechGuru77: wait can the RageBox actually measure signal distance that precisely???TheRealHighwayQueen: destroy them babe show no mercy!!!

"Well, Highway Nation, rules are rules!" Madison's performer instinct took over as she accelerated toward the offending Prius. "Time for some educational content!"

The takedown proceeded flawlessly, with Madison executing a textbook "California Nudge" that sent the Prius spinning onto the shoulder. Their viewers went wild, donations and subscription alerts flooding the screen as Blake narrated the "teaching moment" with practiced authority.

The Prius came to a stop against the guardrail, its hybrid engine sputtering before going silent. A middle-aged man in a rumpled business suit stumbled out, his glasses askew and briefcase contents scattered across the asphalt.

"What is wrong with you people?" he shouted, steadying himself against his vehicle. "I signaled properly! This is insane!"

Madison rolled down her window, her usual fake smile never wavering. "Actually, sir, our RageBox Premium detected that your signal was activated for only 98.7 feet before your lane change. The legal requirement is 100 feet exactly."

"That's impossible!" The man gestured wildly at his car. "That can't be possible! I've been driving for twenty years without a single violation! I'm going to report both of you!"

Blake leaned across Madison, making sure to position perfectly for the camera. "Our Sterling Defense RageBox uses military-grade sensors with point-zero-one accuracy, sir. Maybe upgrade from that prehistoric Prius if you want to avoid further educational moments?"

"I'm a high school science teacher! I understand measurement systems!" The man's face flushed red as he pointed at their SUV. "Your system is rigged to generate content!"

"Sir, we're going to need you to calm down. You've already been cited once today for road rage. I doubt you'd like a second one." Madison said with a snarky tone.

"Especially on a teacher's salary." Blake whispered into her ear.

"I'm calling my lawyer right now!"

Madison fake-whispered to the camera: "Everybody's a scientist until the RageBox receipts come out." She turned back to the man with exaggerated patience. "The RageBox doesn't lie, and the Road Rage Protocol Act Section 4.7 clearly states that disputing an authorized system during an active retaliation window is actually a secondary violation."

"This is highway robbery!" the teacher protested.

"No, sir," Blake corrected with a smirk, "this is highway justice. There's a difference. One's illegal, one is legal content creation."

Their chat exploded:

SterlingDefender: LOL SCIENCE TEACHER JUST GOT SCHOOLEDRoadRage4Life: his face when she quoted the exact section number JusticeServed: these basic drivers always think they know better than premium tech

Madison blew a kiss to the fuming teacher before accelerating away, her tires kicking gravel onto the Prius's already dented hood.

"And that, Highway Nation," Blake announced triumphantly, "is why you always, always maintain your full 100-foot signal distance. Education complete!"

What neither mentioned on camera was how perfectly timed the violation had been—exactly when their viewership typically dipped, precisely when they needed an engagement boost.

Three days later, it happened again.

"RageBox alert!" Blake announced during their afternoon livestream. "Subject vehicle following at 2.9 seconds behind the vehicle ahead. Minimum safe distance is 3.0 seconds—and they have been cited with reckless driving, a Class C offense! Protocol authorizes response!"

Madison again executed the takedown perfectly, but afterward, while pretending to check her makeup in the visor mirror, she whispered, "That's the fourth hair-trigger violation this week, and they're always perfectly timed for when our viewership dips."

Blake maintained his camera smile while replying through clenched teeth. "Don't complain about perfect content opportunities, babe. Just go with it."

Blake shrugged, but privately he'd noticed the same thing. The RageBox seemed to find violations exactly when they needed content. Either they were incredibly lucky, or...

He pushed the thought away. Sterling Defense systems didn't manufacture violations. They couldn't. The liability alone would destroy the company.

But still, the timing was awfully convenient, and if that wasn't weird enough, the pattern continued. A driver going 66 mph in a 65 zone. A turn signal activated for 4.9 seconds instead of the required 5.0 before a lane change. A vehicle straying 0.3 inches over a lane marker. All of them had some sort of minor infraction, compounded by a major one.

Each incident created compelling content. Each take-down drove their ratings higher. But something else was happening, too—the comment sections were becoming increasingly hostile, not just toward their targets, but toward Blake and Madison themselves.

HighwayJustice88: these rich kids are making up violations nowRoadSafety2020: that wasn't even close to a real violationViolationVictim: someone needs to give these two a taste of their own medicineSterlingDefenseInsider: RageBox doesn't even HAVE that level of precision measurement

More concerning were the direct messages—threats from drivers who claimed to be hunting for their distinctive Dominion Motors Conquest Elite SUV. Three times in the past week, they'd spotted vehicles following them after ending their streams, only to disappear when Blake called Sterling Defense security.

"It's getting weird, babe," Madison said one evening, scrolling through their message requests. "Like, engagement and viewership are through the roof, but have you seen these threats? This guy says he's modified his RageBox to specifically target our vehicle signatures."

Blake waved dismissively. "Empty threats from jealous haters. Haters gonna hate. Nobody would dare touch a Sterling Defense vehicle."

"I'm still concerned about this Sarah Foster podcast," Madison said, already pulling up background information.

Blake blew her off. "Nah, we'll just go in and hit our typical talking points and make some epic content."

Madison knew this wasn't a fight worth fighting, so she gave in and nodded.

But Madison still wanted to know what they were getting into. She expected to find the typical profile of an outraged suburban activist with minimal credentials and manufactured outrage. She scrolled through Sarah's social media presence, official biography, and podcast archives, planning to spend no more than fifteen minutes on opposition research. But something caught her attention—a news article about Sarah's daughter Erica, killed in a highway incident two years ago. The story mentioned Sterling Defense products, which prompted Madison to dig deeper, opening multiple search threads and then using Blake's Sterling Defense credentials to compile data from restricted databases that any other influencer wouldn't be able to access.

"This can't be right," Madison muttered three hours later, surrounded by holographic displays in their research room. What had started as basic preparation had turned into a deep dive as she discovered massive discrepancies between Sarah Foster's public persona and Blake's dismissive "Karen" characterization.

Sarah Foster's daughter, Erica, had indeed been killed in a road rage incident two years ago. News reports, court transcripts, and medical examiner records all confirmed it. Sixteen years old. Honor student. Volunteering with a literacy program. She was a passenger in her friend's car when a drunk driver wielding a Sterling Defense "Civilian Protection Kit" had forced them off the road.

Madison pulled up the court case details, her stomach tightening as she read. The drunk driver had claimed the RageBox had authorized his actions after Erica's friend had "committed multiple violations." The case had been dismissed on technical grounds—the RageBox logs were somehow "mysteriously" corrupted, and Sterling Defense had successfully argued that their systems couldn't be held liable for "user implementation decisions."

Most unsettling was the defendant's statement: "The Sterling system told me I was authorized. I was just following protocol."

Madison closed the files, a rare feeling of genuine unease settling over her. This wasn't some random "Karen" looking for attention. Sarah Foster had actually lost her child to the very system Blake and Madison promoted.

"Blake?" she called, her voice unusually small in their cavernous penthouse. "I think we might need to reconsider this podcast."

CHAPTER 3

THE PODCAST

"Welcome to 'Peace in Motion.' I'm your host, Sarah Foster."

Blake and Madison exchanged surprised glances as they settled into surprisingly comfortable chairs in Sarah's studio. They had expected a basement setup with amateur equipment. Instead, they found themselves in a professional-grade studio with multiple cameras, perfect lighting, and a livestream setup that rivaled their own.

Sarah herself was nothing like the shrieking "Karen" they had expected. In her early forties, she had the composed demeanor of someone intimately familiar with trauma. Her simple, elegant clothing projected approachable authority, and her posture—unconsciously straight, feet positioned in a way that suggested tactical training—made Madison curious.

Madison felt her stomach tighten as she studied Sarah's face, but it wasn't about the possible tactical training.

She couldn't help but think of that grieving mother she'd seen in the courthouse photos from two years ago—the woman whose sixteen-year-old daughter had been killed by a drunk driver wielding Sterling Defense equipment, the same equipment that Blake's family manufactured and that Blake and Madison promote on their channel every day.

"Thank you both for coming," Sarah continued, her voice warm and genuine. "I know your schedule must be incredibly demanding with your success."

"We always make time for meaningful dialogue," Blake replied automatically, deploying his pre-planned "generous expert" persona. "Highway safety is literally our passion."

Madison shot Blake a warning glance. He obviously hadn't bothered to read any of the research she'd compiled last night, and so he had no idea who they were really dealing with.

Sarah nodded, her smile reaching her eyes in a way that momentarily disarmed them both. "That's exactly why I wanted to have this conversation. Your journey as content creators has been fascinating—you've really transformed how people think about highway safety and accountability."

Madison blinked, thrown off by the praise. She had prepared for confrontation about Erica's death, not this disarming warmth. "Well, um, yes. We believe in creating educational content that promotes safer driving through, um, deterrence."

"The deterrence model is certainly one approach," Sarah agreed, her tone thoughtful rather than confrontational. "I'd love to hear more about how you developed your philosophy. What inspired you both to focus on highway safety as your platform?"

Blake launched into their standard origin story, relaxing as he hit familiar talking points about "seeing a need for accountability" and "creating content that makes a difference." Madison watched Sarah carefully, noting how the woman's hand briefly touched a small locket hanging around her neck—a locket that Madison now knew likely contained a photo of Erica.

"Your content clearly resonates with millions of people," Sarah observed. "Why do you think that is? What need are you fulfilling for your audience?"

The question seemed innocent enough, but Madison sensed deeper currents. Sarah wasn't just asking about their success—she was probing their understanding of their own influence.

The conversation flowed with unexpected ease. Blake, oblivious to Sarah's true background, shared details about their "mission" with his usual rehearsed confidence. Madison, however, found herself struggling to maintain her performance, hyperaware of every mention of "safety" and "accountability" in light of what she now knew.

"We're really about accountability," Madison said carefully, watching Sarah's reaction. "The highways were chaos before the Protocol."

"Accountability is certainly important," Sarah nodded thoughtfully. "I'm curious, though—have you ever found yourselves in situations where the lines between entertainment and education became blurred?"

Something in her tone—not accusatory, merely curious—prompted unexpected honesty from Blake. "Well, sure, we certainly are trying to entertain folks, but a big part of what drives Madison and myself is the desire to make the road safer for everyone. It's just a bonus that we get to make money doing it."

Madison winced internally. Blake had no idea he was confessing to the mother of a victim.

"That makes sense, I guess. People deserve to get paid for their work," Sarah said, maintaining her professional demeanor despite what Madison imagined must be incredible restraint. "How do you balance that educational mission with the entertainment demands of your platform?"

"It's all about engagement," Blake explained confidently. "Sometimes you need to create moments that capture attention before you can deliver the educational message."

"Create moments," Sarah repeated thoughtfully. "That's fascinating. So some of the violations might be... staged? For maximum educational impact?"

Madison interjected before Blake could dig them into a deeper hole. "We follow strict protocols. Safety is always our priority." She felt the hollowness of her own words, knowing that Sarah's daughter had died because of the very "protocols" she was defending.

"Your family's company provides those protocols, correct?" Sarah asked, her eyes now directly meeting Madison's. "Sterling Defense systems?"

Madison felt a chill. Sarah had known all along who they were—just as Madison now knew who Sarah was. "No, the government developed the protocols, not Sterling Defense."

"But wasn't Sterling Defense the company who lobbied for the new laws?" Sarah asked, her tone remaining conversational despite the pointed question.

"One of the companies, but they don't make laws," Blake replied.

"Yes, but couldn't you see how some people might feel it's like buying laws?" Sarah pressed, leaning forward slightly in her chair.

"No, that is how our government works," Madison interjected firmly, attempting to shut down this line of questioning.

"Yes," Blake admitted, apparently still oblivious to the growing tension. "Sterling Defense's RageBox systems are a part of the process, but that's only because the government felt it was the right product for the job. It's a great product that we use to educate people about safer driving."

"That's interesting," Sarah said, her voice still warm though her eyes never left Madison's. "So your content not only educates but also potentially drives sales for your family business? That's quite synergistic."

"Yeah, it's a win-win," Blake replied defensively. "Better safety technology means safer roads."

"And what about the casualty statistics?" Sarah asked, her tone still conversational. "Sterling Defense publishes quarterly reports on highway violence incidents. The numbers have actually increased by 47% since the Protocol was implemented. How do you reconcile that with your safety mission?"

Madison thought of Erica Foster's autopsy report that she'd read last night, the clinical description of injuries caused by a Sterling Defense-armed driver who claimed he was "just following protocol."

Blake on the other hand had read their research team's brief on Sarah Foster—grief counselor, advocacy work, daughter killed in highway incident. Standard victim profile. What the brief hadn't mentioned was the military precision in her questioning, the way she controlled the conversation like an interrogation—or more importantly, that it was a Sterling Defense system that may have helped lead to her daughter's death.

"Listen, those statistics are complicated," Blake began dismissively.

"Blake," Madison interrupted, unable to maintain the charade any longer. "Ms. Foster lost her daughter to a road rage incident two years ago. Involving Sterling Defense products."

The studio fell silent. Sarah's expression remained professionally composed, but something flickered in her eyes—surprise that Madison had done her research, perhaps.

Blake faltered, his rehearsed persona cracking. "I... I didn't know that. I'm very sorry for your loss."

"Thank you," Sarah replied simply. "Erica was sixteen. The driver who killed her was using a Sterling Defense 'Civilian Protection Kit.' He claimed your family's Rage-Box authorized his actions."

"Oh, I remember this case. The man who," Blake threw up some air quotes for the next part. "claimed our Rage-Box 'authorized his actions'—even though he was also drunk." Blake fell back on some corporate talking points. "You know, our systems don't authorize drunk driving."

"People should drive better if they don't want consequences," Madison said quietly, quoting their standard line, but this time with a hollow, questioning tone—a tacit acknowledgment of its cruel absurdity when faced with Sarah's reality.

"People should drive better if they don't want consequences," Sarah repeated softly. "Would that include sixteen-year-old passengers like Erica?"

On the monitor showing the livestream feed, Madison could see the comment section exploding. Clips of their exchange were already being shared, cut perfectly to expose their callousness rather than celebrate their takedowns.

"We're nearly out of time," Sarah said, maintaining her professionalism despite what must have been intense personal feelings. "Thank you both sincerely for this conversation. It's been incredibly illuminating. My audience and

I appreciate your honesty about your methods, your family connections to Sterling Defense, and your perspectives on highway casualties."

The professional smile never left her face as she wrapped up the interview, thanking them again for their time. As the studio lights dimmed, Sarah approached them with the same warm demeanor she'd maintained throughout.

"That was wonderful," she said, extending her hand. "Truly. You've given my audience exactly what they needed to hear."

"That didn't go as planned," Blake muttered as they exited the studio building. "But I think we salvaged it. You calling that drunk driving the 'consequences' for bad driving was a bit much, but we can spin it."

Madison was already scrolling through their feeds, her expression growing increasingly alarmed. "Blake, this is bad. Really bad. They're cutting clips like we're admitting that we stage violations or something. Your family connection to Sterling is trending. And my stupid 'consequences' comment is everywhere."

"We've weathered controversies before," Blake reassured her, unlocking their vehicle with a gesture. "Remember the school zone incident? Everyone was outraged for like, what—a week? Then we posted that apology video with some donated crossing guard equipment, and our numbers were higher than ever."

Madison wasn't listening. She had gone pale, staring at her phone. "The top comment on our main account is from Sarah Foster. It's just a link."

"Probably some Karen petition. Just ignore it." Blake climbed into the passenger seat, already planning their response strategy.

"It's not a petition." Madison's voice was barely audible. "It's court documents from her daughter's case. The one where a Sterling Defense customer killed her."

Blake froze. "What?"

"She played us, Blake. The whole interview was a set-up to get us to admit on camera that violations can be manufactured and that your family profits from highway violence. She already had the court documents ready to drop the moment we finished."

Before Blake could respond, their SUV's RageBox system suddenly erupted with alerts, the display flashing red with violation notifications.

VIOLATION DETECTED: SPEEDING 28 MPH OVER LIMITVIOLATION DETECTED: FOLLOWING 0.5 SECONDS TOO CLOSELYVIOLATION DETECTED: ILLEGAL LANE CHANGEPROTOCOL AUTHORIZED: CLASS D RESPONSE

"What the—?" Blake stared at the display in confusion.

"Hello! We're not even moving. We're, like, parked!" Madison frantically tapped the override codes, but the system ignored her commands. The parking lot around them was nearly empty—yet according to their RageBox, they were simultaneously committing multiple serious violations.

"Something's wrong with the system," she said, her voice rising with genuine fear. "Call your dad's security team! Now!!!"

Blake reached for his phone just as the first vehicle pulled into the lot—a black sedan with its headlights off. The second arrived from the opposite direction—a pickup truck with reinforced bumpers. Then a third—an SUV nearly identical to their own.

All three vehicles displayed the same glowing red message across their windshields:

PROTOCOL AUTHORIZED

"Blake," Madison whispered with real fear in her voice for the first time since they'd met. "What's happening?"

Blake's eyes darted between the approaching vehicles and their malfunctioning RageBox, which continued to cycle through violations they weren't committing. For once, he had no confident answer, no performance ready, no content strategy prepared.

The vehicles formed a semicircle around them, headlights suddenly flashing on to blind them. Through squinted eyes, Blake could make out the drivers—ordinary-looking people with expressions of grim determination, their RageBoxes all displaying the same message:

TARGET ACQUIRED: STERLING, BLAKE & PERDEW, MADISONVIOLATION CLASS: D+RESPONSE: MAXIMUM FORCE AUTHORIZED

For the first time in their content creation careers, Blake and Madison found themselves on the wrong side of the Protocol—with no cameras running, no audience watching, and no one coming to save them.

CHAPTER 4

THE PURSUIT

A harsh, pulsing alarm blared out of the RageBox. Red emergency lights flashed across the dashboard as a computerized voice filled their luxury SUV:

"ATTENTION: VIOLATION DETECTED. IMMEDIATELY MOVE TO DESIGNATED RAGE LANE FOR PROTOCOL ENFORCEMENT. COMPLIANCE IS MANDATORY. RESISTANCE INCREASES PENALTY SEVERITY."

Madison slammed her manicured hands against the steering wheel. "There is no Rage Lane! We're not even moving!" Her voice cracked with genuine panic—not the manufactured kind she deployed for content reactions; this was real, unfiltered fear.

Blake frantically jabbed at the dashboard controls, the perfect styling of his hair coming undone as sweat beaded on his forehead. The main display flickered, and suddenly they were staring at themselves—not through their carefully positioned ring lights and professional cameras, but from the external perspective of the RageBox network. For the first time in their ragefluencer careers, Blake and Madison Sterling were on the "Violator View" screen.

"This can't be happening," Blake muttered, his carefully cultivated ragefluencer voice abandoned. "The system identifies us as Sterling Defense priority users. It's literally coded into—"

He froze mid-sentence as the pursuing vehicles' driver information populated across their screen. His stomach dropped as he recognized the profile images.

"Babe," Blake whispered. "Road Warrior Randy is driving the pickup. And the Traffic Justice Twins are in the SUV."

Madison's face drained of color. "Our collab partners? But—but we just, like, did that sponsored Dominion event with them last month! They know it's us."

"They're not responding to my messages," Blake said, frantically tapping his phone. "No one is. I've tried my pops, Sterling Defense security, our social team—nothing. I don't understand what's going on. Pop's phone is completely offline, which is impossible since he has a military-grade satellite backup."

Madison's ragefluencer instincts kicked in despite the danger. "We need to livestream this! It's obviously a hilarious glitch, right?" She activated their emergency backup cameras and began broadcasting to their followers. "Hey, Highway Nation! You are not going to believe this, but we're experiencing this crazy system error! Our premium Sterling Defense RageBox thinks we're, like, violators! Can you even believe that? We weren't even moving at the time, so it's, like, obviously a glitch."

Blake nodded enthusiastically, trying to recapture their usual bravado while simultaneously dialing Sterling Defense tech support. "Totally wild technical issue, Highway Nation. Probably just needs a quick system reset or—"

"Sterling Defense technical support, how may I direct your call?" a bored voice finally answered.

"This is Blake Sterling. Yes, that Sterling. We have an emergency override situation. Our RageBox is malfunctioning and identifying us as violators. We need immediate remote system correction and security support." Blake's voice had shifted to the authoritative tone he reserved for service workers and brand representatives who didn't recognize his status.

"I'm sorry, sir, but our systems show no malfunction. Your vehicle has been properly identified under Protocol Amendment Seven, Section Four: 'Repeat violators with documented pattern of malicious noncompliance.' Your violation profile has been distributed to all authorized responders in your vicinity."

"That's impossible! I'm literally a Sterling! My father—"

"Your family status has been temporarily suspended pending investigation. Please comply with all Protocol directives to minimize penalty severity. This call is being recorded for quality assurance."

The line went dead as three more vehicles joined the semicircle surrounding them. Madison's livestream chat was exploding with comments:

TrueRoadWarrior: THIS ISN'T A GLITCH guys this is Amendment 7 enforcement!!!JusticeServd: They're about to get what they deserve finallyHighwayHero42: The Rage Lane system doesn't even activate unless you've had multiple violationsRageLawyer213: GET OFF THE STREAM AND CALL A LAWYER RIGHT NOW

A soccer mom in a minivan pulled up alongside Road Warrior Randy's pickup truck, her display clearly visible through the windshield: "PROTOCOL AUTHORIZED." Behind her, a teenager in a Honda Civic took position, his system showing the same authorization. A retiree in a Buick—complete with golf clubs visible in the back seat—completed the blockade, his weathered face set with determination as his RageBox pulsed with red warning lights.

"Blake, we need to move, or we're getting trapped in here," Madison said, her voice losing its performative edge.

"Then get us out of here, babe!"

Madison slammed her foot down on the accelerator. The Dominion SUV's specialized tires began squealing against the asphalt as she aimed for the narrowest gap between a Buick and Road Warrior Randy's pickup.

"Initiating evasive maneuvers!" she shouted, instinctively falling back on the branded terminology they used in their videos. "Activating Dominion's Tactical Escape System now!"

The SUV sped forward, its military-grade engine roaring to life. For a moment, it seemed they might thread the needle between the vehicles—until Randy's pickup suddenly swerved, deliberately closing the gap.

"He's trying to box us in!" Blake yelled, bracing himself against the dashboard. "Try the other side!"

Madison cranked the wheel hard, the SUV's performance suspension absorbing the g-forces as they changed direction. She spotted another opening between the soccer mom's minivan and the teenager's Civic.

"HOLD ON TO SOMETHING!" she screamed, ramming the accelerator to the floor. The Dominion's front bumper clipped the minivan's rear quarter panel, sending it spinning as they broke through the encirclement.

"That's the Sterling Swift Escape maneuver, Highway Nation!" Blake announced automatically to their livestream, muscle memory taking over despite their genuine terror. "Notice how Madison used the reinforced contact points of our Dominion Elite to—WATCH OUT!"

A projectile—something that looked like a tactical flare—arced through the air and landed directly in front of their vehicle. Madison swerved violently, nearly rolling the SUV as they narrowly avoided the obstacle.

"They're using Sterling Defense Pursuit Deterrents against us!" Madison's voice cracked with irony. "Those things cost $899 for a three-pack! Remember, we promoted 'em last month?"

Blake was holding on for dear life, paying more attention to their current predicament than whether or not they had promoted those dang things.

As they careened toward the parking lot exit, Blake frantically worked the dash controls, trying to override their malfunctioning RageBox. "The system's locked me out completely! We're officially designated as Class D violators with extended retaliation windows!"

The livestream chat was exploding:

JusticeServed: THEY'RE RUNNING!!! Class D penalty just increased by 200%!!!HighwayQueen4Ever:

omg is this real or staged?? best content ever!Violation-Victim: Finally seeing what it feels like on the other sideSterlingDown: All authorized pursuers converging on Wilshire exit now!

"THEY'RE COORDINATING IN THE COMMENTS!" Blake shouted as they burst onto Wilshire Boulevard, the SUV's tires momentarily leaving the ground as they hit the street. "They're using our own livestream to track us!"

"Then shut it down!" Madison barked, her ragefluencer persona completely displaced by genuine fear.

"I CAN'T!" Blake screamed out of frustration as he attempted to shut it down. "THE FREAKIN' RAGE-BOX HAS OVERRIDDEN OUR BROADCASTING SYSTEMS BECAUSE IT THINKS WE'RE CLASS D VIOLATORS!"

A delivery truck suddenly swerved into their lane, its windshield RageBox displaying the glowing authorization. Madison's knuckles whitened as she tightened her grip around the steering wheel.

"HARD RIGHT!" Blake screamed.

Madison cranked the wheel, sending them skidding onto a side street. Behind them, at least five vehicles made the same turn, their headlights forming a predatory convoy in pursuit.

"We need to get to the freeway," Madison said, her voice steadying as she focused on driving. "The Dominion has better top-end speed than anything chasing us."

"Except for Randy's truck—he's got the Sterling Interceptor Package," Blake replied, his eyes glued to the rearview camera feed. "We freakin' literally helped install the dang thing that might help him catch us!"

Madison zigzagged through residential streets, her hands moving with mechanical precision as she utilized every evasive driving technique they'd demonstrated in their highway justice videos. The irony wasn't lost on either of them.

"Freeway entrance coming up in point-three miles," Blake announced, consulting the navigation system. "But there's a problem—the RageBox network has designated all lanes as active Rage Lanes for our pursuit. Every vehicle on the 405 will be authorized to engage us."

"Then we gotta go somewhere else," Madison countered, swerving around a corner so sharply that Blake's head smacked up against the window.

"Where? The entire RageBox network has us flagged! There's nowhere in the city we can—" Blake froze mid-sentence, his eyes widening in sudden realization. "The analog district! East Hollywood, baby!"

Madison shot him a confused glance. "Really!?! Ugh!"

"Pops always called it a 'regulatory oversight zone.' No RageBox sensors, no protocol enforcement!"

Madison nodded grimly, calculating the route in her head. "East Hollywood it is. But we've got to, like, lose these guys first."

She spotted their opportunity ahead—a busy intersection with a stale green light. Flooring the accelerator, the Dominion SUV rocketed forward, weaving between cars waiting to turn left.

"Hang on!" Madison shouted as she blew through the intersection just as the light turned red. Behind them, their pursuers faced a wall of cross-traffic—but to her horror, they didn't stop. Road Warrior Randy's pickup plowed directly into a sedan, shoving it aside as the others followed, authorized by their RageBoxes to continue pursuit regardless of traffic signals.

"WHAT THE HECK, MAN!" Blake screamed out, watching the carnage in their wake. "They're using Amendment Seven provisions. Full pursuit authorization regardless of secondary casualties! Brutal!"

The freeway entrance loomed ahead, and Madison made a split-second decision. "We can't lead them into regular traffic. Too many people will get hurt."

She yanked the wheel, sending them onto a parallel access road that ran alongside the 405. Their pursuers adjusted immediately, the convoy now swelling to at least eight vehicles.

"They're using the Sterling Swarm Protocol," Blake realized, watching their tactical positioning. "Classic pincer formation with staggered pursuit vehicles."

"I guess you should know," Madison snapped, her focus entirely on keeping them alive now. "Since you, like, narrated the training video!"

The access road narrowed, forcing Madison to slow as they approached a construction zone. Behind them, Randy's pickup had closed the gap, its reinforced bumper now just yards from their rear.

"He's going to ram us," Blake warned, bracing himself against the dashboard.

CRASH! The impact came with brutal force, Madison's specialized driver seat absorbing much of the shock as the Dominion SUV fishtailed wildly. She fought for control, expertly counter-steering as Randy backed off for another strike.

"Our rear defensive systems activated," Blake turned to her, waiting for her response. "Countermeasures available."

"Deploy smoke!" Madison ordered, her voice steady despite the situation.

Blake slammed his palm against a red button on the console. From beneath their SUV, specialized smoke canisters released a thick gray cloud, temporarily blinding their pursuers. The Traffic Justice Twins vehicle swerved violently, nearly colliding with the concrete barrier.

"It won't stop them for long," Blake warned as Madison pushed the SUV to its limits, the speedometer climbing past 90 mph on the narrow access road.

Sure enough, headlights soon pierced the smoke behind them, the pursuit vehicles emerging in a tight formation. But now something else joined the chase—police helicopters circling overhead, their spotlights sweeping the road.

"Great, even the cops are after us now!" Madison's voice cracked with stress as she swerved to avoid debris on the road.

"No, look!" Blake pointed upward as one of the helicopters banked sharply. "They're not following us—they're trying to coordinate traffic breaks to minimize civilian casualties from our pursuers. The entire city is watching this chase!"

Their livestream chat confirmed it:

NewsAlert: BREAKING: Ragefluencers Blake Sterling and Madison Perdew in high-speed pursuit, 405 shut down, 7 vehicles involvedTrafficAuthority: ALL DRI-

VERS AVOID WESTSIDE, major pursuit incident in progressRageBoxUpdate: System shows 23 additional authorized pursuers en route to intercept

Suddenly Madison could see construction equipment blocking the access road a few yards ahead, giving her seconds to decide what to do—slam on the brakes or find another way.

"There!" Blake pointed to a partially constructed off-ramp. "Construction access!"

Madison didn't hesitate. She yanked the wheel hard, sending the SUV bouncing over a dirt berm and onto the unfinished ramp. The Dominion's specialized suspension compressed to its limits as they caught air, landing with a bone-jarring impact on the rough concrete surface.

"Tire pressure warning!" Blake shouted as alerts flashed across their dash. "Left rear is compromised!"

"Dominion's Run-Flat system can handle it," Madison replied through gritted teeth, fighting to keep the vehicle stable on the uneven surface. "We've got twenty miles before critical failure."

Behind them, only three vehicles made the jump successfully—Randy's pickup and two others. The rest skidded to a halt at the construction barrier, forced to find alternate routes.

"We've thinned the herd," Blake observed, a hint of his old confidence returning. "Now we just need to—"

CRASH! A deafening impact rocked the SUV as Randy's pickup connected with their rear bumper at high speed. The Dominion's frame groaned in protest as Madison struggled to maintain control on the unfinished ramp.

"He's executing a Sterling Takedown!" Blake's voice rose in pitch. "Our signature move!"

Madison countered instinctively, the thousands of hours spent performing takedowns for content now serving her as she fought to avoid becoming a victim of the same technique. She feathered the brakes, letting Randy's pickup surge forward alongside them, then sharply accelerated as he attempted to turn into their vehicle.

"The PIT maneuver only works if your target behaves predictably," Madison muttered, reciting from their own training videos as she outdrove the technique.

Up ahead, they could see the unfinished ramp was coming to an abrupt end, dropping off into emptiness where construction had yet to connect it to the cross street below. Madison slammed on the brakes, the SUV's performance braking system screaming as they skidded toward the edge.

"We're not going to stop in time!" Blake shouted, genuine terror in his voice.

Madison cranked the wheel at the last possible moment, sending them into a controlled slide that brought them to a halt mere inches from the drop-off. Behind them, Randy wasn't so lucky, his pickup's momentum carrying it past them and over the edge. The vehicle crashed onto the street twenty feet below, its specialized safety systems deploying instantly to protect the driver.

"One down," Madison breathed, hands shaking on the wheel. The remaining two pursuit vehicles had halted a safe distance behind them, momentarily trapped in the standoff.

"We need to find another way down," Blake said, frantically studying the navigation system. "We're sitting ducks up here."

Madison reversed carefully, keeping their pursuers at bay with the threat of collision.

"Babe, just two blocks to freedom! Just keep heading east and we'll hit the analog district!" Blake turned to see what was going on behind them.

The pursuit vehicles began to accelerate, ending Blake and Madison's temporary reprieve.

"We need to go now!" Panic was beginning to bleed into Blake's voice.

Madison put the SUV back into gear and slammed on the gas. "Okay, two blocks east. Blake, guide me!"

Blake frantically pulled up satellite imagery of the area. "Um... Okay... Got it! There's a service road coming up. It should get us out of here. Hard left... now!"

Madison spun the wheel, the SUV's tires spinning on loose gravel as they careened down a steep, unpaved track. Their specialized suspension worked overtime, absorbing impacts that would have disabled any normal vehicle as they bounced and slid toward street level.

Behind them, only one pursuit vehicle managed to follow—a heavy-duty SUV driven by one of the Traffic Justice Twins. The other remained stuck at the top of the ramp, unable to navigate the treacherous descent.

"They're still on us!" Blake shouted, watching the rearview camera. "And the RageBox is showing more authorized pursuers converging on our position from all directions!"

The service road deposited them onto a side street, where Madison immediately gunned the engine, sending them hurtling toward what looked like an invisible boundary two blocks ahead. The streets here were noticeably different—fewer cameras, more potholes, older buildings with no smart infrastructure visible.

"There it is," Blake pointed frantically. "The analog district starts at that intersection!"

Like it was cued up ready for Blake to finish, the RageBox warning notification kicked in: "ATTENTION: YOU ARE NEARING THE ANALOG DISTRICT. IN ACCORDANCE WITH SECTION VII OF THE ROAD RAGE PROTOCOL ACT, SURVEILLANCE IS PROHIBITED BY FEDERAL LAW. RAGEBOX ENFORCEMENT DOES NOT APPLY IN THE ANALOG DISTRICT. ANY VIOLATION WILL BE PROSECUTED TO THE FULLEST EXTENT OF THE LAW."

The Traffic Justice Twins SUV was still right behind them, gaining ground with each second. As they approached the intersection, the pursuer made one final desperate attempt, accelerating alongside them and swerving sharply to force them into a parked car.

Madison reacted instinctively, dropping back and then accelerating through the narrow gap between the pursuit vehicle and the row of parked cars. Metal screeched against metal as their SUV scraped past with no room to spare.

"We made it!" Blake shouted as they crossed the invisible line into the analog district.

"RAGEBOX DEACTIVATED." The RageBox warning notification spit out before the dashboard displays went dark on the RageBox system.

Behind them, their pursuer skidded to a halt exactly at the boundary, unwilling to follow into territory where they would face arrest for their actions. Through the rearview mirror, they could see the driver—one of the Traffic Justice Twins—glaring at them from behind his steering wheel, rage evident even at a distance.

"I can't believe we made it," Madison gasped, her hands trembling as she guided their damaged SUV deeper into the analog district. "We actually made it."

The transformation around them was immediate and disorienting. After years of living in a world where every inch of road was monitored, measured, and monetized, the sudden absence felt like diving underwater. The streets here had a different energy—people walked without constantly checking devices, cars moved with consideration rather than calculation, and not a single promotional billboard tracked their eyeline with personalized content.

"I've never actually gone into a historical preservation zone before. It feels..." Blake struggled to find the words, his ragefluencer vocabulary suddenly inadequate, "...real. Like—like we've gone back in time."

Madison nodded, noticing how her heartbeat was gradually slowing. "No wonder your father's company lobbied so hard against these places. There's no money to be made when people just... drive normally."

"Yeah, they sort of had to let places like this go to get the Road Rage Protocol passed as a law." Blake shrugged off the thought. "I guess this is what you get when the law prohibits installing an infrastructure that would 'alter the character' of the neighborhood. You know, Pops would never let me come to places like this because he said he'd have no way to track me if I got kidnapped or something."

For the first time in years, they traveled without performing for an audience, their actions no longer translating into content, metrics, or engagement statistics. The silence of an analog existence was terrifying—yet strangely liberating.

Blake slumped in his seat, the adrenaline draining from his system as the immediate danger passed. All around them, the neighborhood looked alien to their privileged eyes—no smart streetlights, no visible evidence of the technological infrastructure they took for granted.

"What now?" Madison asked, her voice small in the sudden quiet of their vehicle.

Blake stared out at the unfamiliar landscape, at the people walking freely without the constant surveillance they'd known their entire lives.

"I don't know," he admitted, the weight of their situation finally sinking in. "I really don't know."

CHAPTER 5

GOING ANALOG

The Dominion SUV limped deeper into the analog district, its once-pristine matte-black finish now scarred with deep gouges and impact dents. The specialized run-flat tires had finally given out, the right rear rubber shredded to tatters, slapping against the wheel well with each rotation. Without the RageBox system's constant digital hum, the vehicle felt eerily quiet—almost ghost-like.

"We can't keep driving this thing," Madison said, her perfectly manicured nails chipped and broken from gripping the steering wheel during their escape. "It's too, like, recognizable. Everyone in the city is probably looking for us, illegal or not. And I'm sure with all the carnage we just left behind, the cops are after us, too."

Blake stared blankly at the darkened dashboard displays. The military-grade screens that had once shown their livestream metrics, violation authorizations, and sponsorship analytics were now just reflective black glass. He tapped his phone again—no signal. He knew what that meant.

"Babe, they cut us off."

"What did you expect? We're, like, fugitives now."

"I—I've never been this... uh, disconnected before," Blake whispered, fear creeping into his voice. "Ugh, that means no platinum credit cards either."

"And your Sterling family name is more of a liability rather than an asset."

"Double ugh."

Madison guided the vehicle into an abandoned warehouse lot, killing the engine. The silence that followed was deafening. No notification chimes. No livestream comments. No algorithm-generated advice on their next content opportunity.

"We need to ditch everything," she said, surprising herself with how quickly her survival instincts had overridden her ragefluencer persona. "Our phones, the SUV, our cards—anything with tracking capabilities."

"But my followers—" Blake started automatically.

"—will watch us die if we try to reconnect," Madison cut him off sharply. "Someone has turned, like, the entire system against us. Every ragefluencer in the country is hunting us now."

Blake ran his fingers through his once-perfectly styled hair, now matted with sweat. "My pops will fix this. He literally owns the company that makes the RageBoxes, so he'll know what to do."

"Your father hasn't answered a single call," Madison reminded him, her voice hardening. "Either he can't help us or—"

"—or he won't," Blake finished, the reality of their situation finally sinking in.

They abandoned the SUV behind the warehouse, taking only what they could carry in a single backpack—some cash Madison had kept "for aesthetic purposes" in her content about financial responsibility, a few protein bars from their sponsored emergency kit, and a paper map of Los Angeles that had been stuffed in the glove compartment as a vintage prop for one of their "retro road rage" themed videos.

The streets of the analog district felt alien to them. No sleek autonomous vehicles, no digital signage that recognized them, no priority access lanes or VIP zones. Just ordinary people driving pre-2020 cars without combat modifications or tactical upgrades.

"None of these cars have armored plating," Blake noticed as they walked along a busy street. "I mean, how do they survive without defense systems?"

"By not attacking each other in the first place," Madison replied quietly. "Look—no one's trying to force anyone off the road or create 'educational content' at each other's expense."

"You say it like it's a bad thing." Blake joked, not reading the room.

"Well, isn't it, you know, like, a bad thing!?! Look where it got us!"

"Whoa, is Aunt Fl—"

"Blake, you better not finish what you're about to say."

Luckily, Blake knew better, and they wandered through the neighborhood silently as darkness fell. The unfamiliar sensation of anonymity was both terrifying and surprisingly liberating. No one recognized them here. No one cared about their follower count or engagement metrics. They were just two scared young people with no idea how to navigate a world without digital validation.

"We need somewhere to sleep," Madison said, eyeing the darkening sky. "And food. Real food, not just those protein bars."

Blake pulled out his wallet, extracting several hundred-dollar bills. "This should get us a decent hotel room, at least."

Madison shook her head. "Luxury hotels require ID verification through the network. Besides, they'll be the first place they look for us."

"Then what about—"

"Cash-only motels. The kind of places that don't ask questions," Madison interrupted, surprising Blake with her knowledge. "I researched them once for a 'slumming it' content series we never filmed."

They found a run-down motel with a flickering neon "VACANCY" sign at the edge of the district. The front desk clerk—an elderly man who didn't even glance up—seemed utterly unimpressed by Blake's attempt to slip him an extra hundred for a "premium room."

"All rooms same. Seventy cash per night. No room service. No Wi-Fi. Pay phone in lobby if you need it," he stated flatly, sliding a physical key across the counter. An actual metal key, not a digital access card or biometric scanner.

Blake mouthed "What the—" to Madison as he grabbed the key.

Their room was small, bare, and smelled faintly of disinfectant. The bed squeaked under their weight as they sat side by side, staring at the blank wall where a smart display would normally be.

"Um... I'm not sure if I can live like this," Blake admitted, his voice small and vulnerable in a way Madison had never heard before. "I've never... I mean, I've literally never been off-grid. Not once in my entire life."

"You never went camping?"

"No. My idea of camping would be a nice ski resort or something."

Madison took a deep breath. "Well, love, you're in for, like, a big surprise then."

Madison reached for his hand, their fingers intertwining without the usual positioning for optimal camera angles. "Don't worry. We'll figure it out. One step at a time."

They barely slept, the unfamiliar sounds of analog life—cars without noise suppression, neighbors with actual conversations rather than digital entertainment—keeping them on edge all night.

Morning came with harsh sunlight through the ever-so-thin curtains. It was a rude awakening for them. No more blackout curtains to block out the sun from messing with the screens that littered their previous life. No more programmed circadian lighting system.

"Ah, man, turn it off." Blake swatted at the sunlight as he awoke from a daze that had him briefly forgetting where he was.

"Let me get right on that, Blake."

"Huh?"

"That's, like, the sun, and the curtains are closed, so I don't know what else I could do."

"Whatever." He grabbed her pillow and covered his head with it.

Madison lifted it out of his sleepy hands. "Blake, we need to get up and figure this out. And we need, like, different clothes." Madison examined her designer outfit now smudged with dirt and torn in their escape. "These scream 'privileged ragefluencer' from like a mile away."

They found their solution at a discount clothing store the motel clerk had suggested. They rummaged through the rack searching for anything that might blend in with their new surroundings—generic jeans, t-shirts, and hoodies—the kind of "basic" apparel they would have mocked mercilessly in their content. Blake stared at the price tags in genuine shock.

"Twenty dollars for jeans? I mean, how do they make any profit margin on these?"

"I don't know. Maybe by not embedding tactical reinforcement or brand authentication chips," Madison replied, already adapting faster than he was. Her ragefluencer affectations were dropping away by the hour, revealing a person that Blake had never seen before.

They were learning new things about each other, and both enjoyed their newfound dynamics: Madison became the dominant one, which Blake found he quite liked. And Madison loved the fact that Blake would follow her suggestions—oh, who was she kidding—orders.

They spent the day learning the basics of analog existence—how to navigate without GPS, how to use paper money for small purchases, how to blend in with ordinary people who weren't performing for cameras or sponsors.

Blake struggled with even the simplest tasks. "What do you mean I have to pump my own gas?" he asked incredulously when they stopped at a station to fill a gas can for their eventual escape from the city. "I mean, don't they have service attendants here?"

"Not in this reality," Madison replied, demonstrating the process she'd only ever performed for "relatable content" segments. "Just squeeze the handle and watch the numbers."

"But how does it know how to charge my account?"

"It doesn't. And besides, don't you remember that we have to pay in cash right now? You have to, like, go inside, you know, and hand the money to an actual human person."

Blake looked genuinely lost. "But what about my reward points? You know I love my reward points."

"I know, baby. But you really have enough money where rewards don't matter, don't you think?"

"It's not the same." Blake pouted.

Madison just nodded her head. "I know. I know. You feel like you really have to work for it."

"Exactly! You so get me, babe!" Blake smiled.

As evening approached, they felt more confident in their disguises and ventured out for food, finding a small diner that advertised "No Digital Menu—Just Good Food" in its window. The waitress didn't scan them for preference profiles or offer personalized upsells. Nope, she just handed them some good ol' fashioned laminated menus and asked what they wanted.

"Wow, this place is so authentic," Blake whispered, as if discovering an exotic culture. "I've seen stuff like this in the movies, but this is like we're in a historical reenactment."

Halfway through their meal, Madison suddenly froze, her fork clattering to her plate. Through the window, she spotted a massive black truck pulling up directly across from their diner. Its windows were tinted completely black, making it impossible to see who was inside.

"Blake," she hissed, nudging him under the table. "Look up slowly. I think someone's found us."

Blake carefully raised his eyes, his heart sinking at the sight of the menacing vehicle. It was even more heavi-

ly modified than their Dominion SUV had been—reinforced bumpers, specialized tactical tires, and what looked
like military-grade defensive plating.

"How did they find us?" he whispered, already calculating escape routes. "We ditched everything with tracking
capabilities."

"I don't know, but we need to move. Like now."

They left cash on the table and slipped out the diner's
back exit, cutting through an alley to reach their motel.
Madison peered around the corner before cursing under
her breath.

"Of course, the truck is out here now. How'd they know
where we'd be?"

Blake's eyes widened. "What if they're tracking us
through the analog surveillance network? Street cameras,
traffic systems—"

"None of that's connected to the RageBox network,"
Madison countered, but uncertainty crept into her voice.
"Wait, are they?"

As if answering her question, the truck's horn suddenly
blared—three short bursts that could only be meant for
them. The message was clear: we see you.

"Run!" Blake grabbed Madison's hand, and they bolted
down the street, ducking between buildings and through
parking lots, using every evasive technique they'd learned

from years of creating chase content—except this time, their lives actually depended on it.

The truck appeared at every turn with the engine growling like a predator, its headlights sweeping across them as they desperately sought escape. It never attempted to run them down directly, instead it herded them like a sheepdog, cutting off escape routes and forcing them deeper into the analog district.

"It's like they're toying with us," Madison gasped as they crouched behind a dumpster, trying to catch their breath. "Why not just run us over and, like, be done with it?"

"Maybe they want us alive," Blake suggested grimly. "You know, so they can make an example out of us with a public execution or something."

"Way to lighten the mood."

"What?! Do you have any better ideas on why?"

"No."

"So grim it is then."

The truck's headlights swept past their hiding spot, momentarily blinding them before continuing down the street. They were able to catch their breath for a precious few seconds as they ducked into an alley.

"Let's double back," Madison whispered. "Try to reach the boundary of the district. Maybe we can—"

The truck's engine roared to life behind them, blocking their only means of escape.

"I guess this is it, babe." Blake muttered as they turned around to face the truck. "At least there aren't any cameras to record our final moments. No embarrassing death compilation videos."

"Speak for yourself," Madison replied, her eyes never leaving the truck as its driver's door swung open. "I always thought I'd go out with at least a million viewers watching live."

CHAPTER 6

CONSEQUENCES

A figure emerged from the truck—tall, muscular, with a thick beard and eyes hidden behind tactical sunglasses despite the darkness. He wore no logos, no sponsored apparel, nothing that could identify him.

"Well, if it isn't Blake Sterling and Madison Perdew," the man called out, his voice echoing in the narrow alley. "The highway's golden couple. Not so golden now, are ya?"

Blake stepped forward slightly, instinctively putting himself between Madison and the stranger. "Look, if you're going to kill us, just get it over with. But if there's a bounty or something, maybe we can work something out. My family has resources—"

"Your family," the man cut him off, "doesn't even know where you are right now. And neither does anyone else in the system." He reached up and removed his sunglasses, revealing a face that both Blake and Madison instantly recognized.

"Derek Santos?" Madison gasped, recognizing the former star of "Road Rage Revolution," one of the most popular ragefluencer channels before its mysterious shutdown a year earlier. "We all thought you were dead!"

Derek's laugh held no humor. "Yeah, I've gotten that before. That's what the algorithm wants you to believe. I was forced out, much like you, except in my case Road Rage Revolution wasn't real—it was my cover story."

Blake and Madison exchanged uncertain glances.

"Cover for what?" Blake asked.

"To fight corporate espionage. I'm a cybersecurity consultant hired by your father to infiltrate Nexus operations." Derek checked his surroundings. "My ragefluencer persona was designed to get close to their recruitment networks. Your father's been investigating security vulnerabilities for well over a year now." He gestured toward his truck. "Look, I'll explain it all once we're safe, but we ain't safe out here. So how about you both get in before that kill squad Nexus sent gets here."

"Kill squad!?!" Blake yelled, before he realized he probably shouldn't be yelling it. "Kill squad?" he whispered.

"Yep. They're maybe twenty minutes behind us." Derek looked at his watch. "Maybe less."

"Dude, how old are you?" Blake asked while staring at Derek's watch.

"Blake, we really don't have time for this." Madison tried to push him along and into the truck.

"Babe. I'm not moving until I know how he found us," Blake demanded, refusing to move toward the truck.

"The same way I stayed alive after my cancellation," Derek replied, checking his watch impatiently. "I saw your takedown happening in real-time. The whole system is buzzing about it. Sterling Defense's golden boy and his trophy fiancée, finally getting a taste of their own medicine. It's trending in thirty-two countries."

Madison's face hardened at the "trophy fiancée" comment, but survival instincts overrode her pride. "Then why, like, help us? We were competitors. You always acted like you hated us."

"Correction: I hated what we *all* represented," Derek said, his expression darkening. "But right now, we need to move. That escape of yours? It made you famous in a whole new way. Every ragefluencer with something to prove is hunting you now."

A distant engine roar punctuated his warning. Derek jerked his head toward his truck. "Last chance. In or out?"

Blake and Madison shared a final glance before making their choice—which was pretty obvious since they really only had one.

The truck's interior was nothing like they expected—no luxury features, no tactical displays, no social media integration. Instead, it was stripped down to essentials, with reinforced seating, basic controls, and what looked like homemade defensive systems.

"Welcome to the analog district," Derek said as he pulled away from the alley, driving with a precision that spoke of his experience. "Hope you're ready to learn how the other half lives."

"Yeah, yeah, we've already seen it. Been there, done that. Right now, I really just need to know what's going on," Blake pleaded.

"Nexus has been systematically eliminating social media personalities who promote Sterling Defense products. Some through discreditation campaigns, others through arranged 'accidents,'" Derek explained, eyes constantly checking the rearview mirror with practiced vigilance.

"That's crazy," Blake protested as he ran his fingers anxiously through his disheveled hair. "Nexus and Sterling are competitors, sure, but they're both legitimate defense contractors."

Derek's eyes briefly met Blake's. "You know how much money there is in militarized civilian vehicles, don't you?" he asked.

"Yes, but—"

"There is no but," Derek interrupted. "Your father built Sterling Defense to dominate the market, and Nexus was having a hard time breaking in legally, so—"

This time Madison interrupted."—so they did whatever they could."

"Yep—by any means necessary. Their plan is to create a crisis, then position themselves as the solution. Highway violence is a billion-dollar market," Derek explained. "And Sterling Defense controls the vast majority of it. Nexus tried competing legitimately for years, but as you know, it really wasn't a competition. Nothin' they did worked, so they decided to go another route and manufacture a crisis that would discredit Sterling Defense and set themselves up as the only choice. Didn't ya'll notice that your system was acting a lil' funky?"

"We did have a bunch of hair-trigger violations that were oddly timed with our viewership dips," Blake admitted, his eyes widening with realization as the pieces started to fall into place.

"And the RageBox started using decimal points," Madison added.

"Those precision measurements were fake," Derek continued. "Real RageBox systems can't measure signal distances to decimal points—the sensors aren't that accurate.

But Nexus's spoofing device can program any violation it wants, down to fake precision measurements."

"I don't understand. How did they hack our RageBox?" Blake asked, his brow furrowed in confusion as he tried to process the implications of what Derek was telling them.

Derek pulled out a small device. "They didn't hack it. They spoofed it. This transmitter mimics RageBox authority signals—makes every system in range think there's a legitimate violation in progress."

Madison stared at the device. "That's impossible. Sterling Defense systems have authentication protocols—"

"Protocols that Nexus helped design," Derek interrupted. "Between that device and Nexus selling 'upgraded' RageBox components with backdoors built in, they've been able to manufacture a lot of false errors designed to make Sterling look like the villain while Nexus swoops in to save the day as the responsible alternative."

Then the realization hit Madison. "Wait, were they, like, responsible for killing Sarah's daughter?"

Derek nodded his head and took a deep breath. "We think they are. And you know about her group Citizens Against Highway Violence, right?"

Blake and Madison both nodded.

"Well, they're funded entirely by Nexus. They're trying to build a case to blame the entire highway violence epidemic on Sterling Defense, then introduce their 'safer, smarter' civilian defense systems as the solution."

Madison's mind raced, connections forming rapidly. "Wait, Sarah Foster, and her podcast—"

"Is part of the operation," Derek confirmed. "Though I'm not sure Foster herself knows anything about it. Her grief is real—her daughter really did die. But Nexus found her, cultivated her, positioned her as the perfect weapon against Sterling."

Blake sank deeper into his seat. "This is insane. You're telling me my family's company is being set up as a scapegoat by Nexus?"

"Yep, all for the next phase," Derek explained. "Military-grade autonomous defense systems in every vehicle. No human control. No override options. Complete surveillance and compliance enforcement."

Blake threw his hands outward from his temples, fingers splayed in the universal 'mind blown' gesture, his eyes wide with disbelief.

"I know, right?" Madison nodded her head in agreement.

Derek drove them deep into the heart of the analog district, eventually arriving at what appeared to be an abandoned auto repair shop. The garage door rolled up automatically as they approached, then closed immediately behind them.

Inside, Blake and Madison found themselves in another world. Dozens of pre-2020 vehicles lined the massive space, each modified in ways that would never pass Sterling Defense inspection. Men and women worked on engines, communication equipment, and what looked like jammers and countermeasures.

"What is this place?" Blake asked, taking in the operation with wide eyes.

"Home," Derek replied simply, leading them past curious onlookers toward a central planning area. "For all of us who've been erased from the system."

A large map of Los Angeles dominated the wall, with analog markers indicating safe zones, danger areas, and patrol routes. Around it stood a diverse group of people who all shared one common feature—recognition flashed in their eyes when they saw Blake and Madison.

"These are the Analog Drivers," Derek explained, gesturing to the group. "Former ragefluencers, engineers, regular people who got caught in the system's crosshairs. We all have one thing in common—Nexus Defense Systems tried to erase us."

"They need to eliminate the old guard first," a woman explained. "People like you, Blake. Your father. Anyone associated with the 'flawed' first generation of highway justice systems."

Blake looked up, his face pale. "So my father is in danger, too?"

Derek nodded solemnly. "Yep."

Madison moved to Blake's side, her hand finding his shoulder in genuine support. "What do we do now? We can't go back into the system, so we can't contact anyone to warn them or for help."

"First," Derek said, "you both need to learn to survive offline. Madison, you need to relearn how to drive without Sterling Defense products—real driving, not performance driving for content. Blake, you need to learn how to navigate without GPS, communicate without digital networks, and exist without constant validation of your identity—or loads of money."

"Oh, come on guys, I can do those things," Blake protested weakly.

Derek raised an eyebrow. "Really? When's the last time you pumped gas? Bought food with cash? Read a paper map? Fixed something instead of replacing it? Drove a car without sixteen automated defense systems?"

Blake shrugged. "I mean, technically, I did some of those things today."

"Yeah, I bet," Derek looked him right in his eyes. "But you struggled, didn't ya?"

"Well—" Blake just trailed off, dropping his eyes to the ground.

"Your privileged upbringing is now your biggest liability," Derek continued without mercy. "Out here, your family name means nothing. Your follower count means nothing. Your only value is what you can contribute and what you can learn."

Madison straightened her spine, a determination hardening in her eyes that had nothing to do with content creation or performance. "Then teach us. Whatever we need to know to survive—and let's stop these people."

Derek studied her for a moment before nodding with grudging respect. "We start now. Because in three days, we're infiltrating the abandoned military base that houses Citizens Against Highway Violence."

"Why three days?" Blake asked, standing to join Madison.

"Because that's when Sarah Foster is scheduled to meet with your father," Derek replied grimly. "And if our intelligence is correct, it won't be for an interview."

The revelation hung heavy in the air as Blake and Madison exchanged alarmed glances. Their world had been completely upended, their identities stripped away, their privilege rendered meaningless. Yet somehow, in this underground garage filled with analog outcasts, they suddenly felt more genuine purpose than they had in years of creating "educational content."

"So, like, where do we begin?" Madison asked, her ragefluencer affect completely gone, now replaced by sincere resolve.

"With lesson one," Derek replied, tossing her a set of keys to an ancient, unmodified sedan. "How to drive without letting an algorithm decide who lives and who dies."

Madison struggled for a bit with the mechanical demands of truly analog driving—no targeting assistance, no automated defensive measures, no threat assessment algorithms. Her precision behind the wheel had once been the envy of the ragefluencer community, but now she had to rebuild it from the ground up.

"You're still driving like you're filming content," Derek criticized after her fourth failed attempt at a basic evasive maneuver. "Stop performing, and start surviving."

Blake faced even greater challenges as he struggled with the analog equipment, not because he was incompetent, but because everything he'd learned was automated. "I know how to drive," he protested, "but I've never had to do it without targeting assistance, threat assessment, route optimization..."

"That's the point," Derek explained. "You've been driving with training wheels your entire life. Time to learn balance."

"Who are you, Mr. Miyagi or something?" Blake joked.

"Ya keep that up, I will have you washing and waxing the cars."

"Dang, dude, I was just playing around."

"That's the problem. Ya haven't needed to survive before." Derek paused, not really wanting to say the next part. "I'd hate to break it to ya, Blake, but playtime is over. Your life is on the line now."

Blake took a deep breath. "Okay."

"Okay?"

"Yeah."

"Great, let's get ya going."

The next three days passed in a blur of intensive training.

On the morning of the third day, Derek gathered them for the final briefing. The plan was audacious but simple: infiltrate the abandoned military base where Citizens Against Highway Violence had established their headquarters, confirm the Nexus connection, and extract Blake's father if needed.

"Intel suggests Foster is planning something big," Derek explained, pointing to surveillance photos taken by people using cameras with telephoto lenses, not network-connected drones. "Multiple tactical vehicles have entered the compound in the last twenty-four hours. Security has tripled."

"How do we get in?" Madison asked, studying the compound layout.

"The old-fashioned way," Derek replied with a grim smile. "We drive right through the front gate."

The plan relied on the one advantage they still possessed—Nexus wouldn't expect Blake Sterling to return willingly to the very people hunting him. The element of surprise, combined with analog vehicles that wouldn't register on the base's RageBox detectors, might just give them the edge they needed.

As night fell, a convoy of five unmarked vehicles—all pre-2020 models with specialized modifications—departed the Analog Drivers' headquarters. Blake and Madison rode with Derek in his truck, their hearts pounding with a different kind of adrenaline than they'd ever experienced making content.

"Remember," Derek cautioned as they approached the darkened military base, "once we're inside, we're on our own. No backup, no extraction plan if things go sideways. We get in, confirm the connection, find your father if he's there, and get out. Nothing more. Nothing less."

Blake nodded, his face set with determination. "I'm ready."

The gate never stood a chance. Derek's truck, modified with an electromagnetic pulse generator designed specifically to disable Sterling and Nexus security systems, knocked out the perimeter defenses long enough for their convoy to slip through. They abandoned the vehicles in a maintenance yard and proceeded on foot, using the compound map Derek's team had painstakingly assembled.

"The main building is ahead," Derek whispered as they crouched behind a storage container. "That's where the activity's been centered."

Blake peered through the darkness at the nondescript building that supposedly housed Citizens Against Highway Violence. Nothing about its exterior suggested the corporate conspiracy Derek had described—it looked exactly like what it claimed to be, a nonprofit advocacy organization working from repurposed military offices.

"Are you sure about this?" he whispered to Derek. "It doesn't look like they can do much, you know."

Derek pointed to a row of vehicles parked behind the building—tactical SUVs with specialized equipment visible even from a distance. "Those aren't standard issue for grief counselors."

They moved silently toward the main building's entrance, using the analog night vision goggles Derek had provided. The door's security system fell to another EMP burst, and they slipped inside, finding themselves in a darkened reception area decorated with highway safety posters and memorial photographs of accident victims.

"This way," Derek directed, consulting his hand-drawn map. "According to the building plans, there should be a conference room down this hallway."

They moved cautiously through the silent building, passing offices that genuinely appeared to be dedicated to highway safety advocacy—budget spreadsheets for awareness campaigns, educational materials, support group schedules. Madison began to wonder if Derek's conspiracy theory was just that—a theory, born of paranoia after being forced off the grid.

Then they reached the conference room.

The door was slightly ajar, a sliver of light spilling into the hallway. Derek held up a hand, signaling them to wait as he peered through the gap. His body tensed immediately.

"Blake," he whispered, his voice tight. "You need to see this."

Blake edged forward and looked through the opening. The conference room had been transformed into what could only be described as a tactical operations center. Digital displays covered the walls, showing Sterling Defense facilities, executive profiles, and what appeared to be attack scenarios. Armed personnel in unmarked tactical gear moved efficiently around the space, checking weapons and equipment.

And at the center of it all stood Sarah Foster, no longer playing the role of grieving counselor. She was dressed in combat fatigues, directing operations with the confidence of someone well-versed in military procedures. But what froze Blake's blood was the sight directly behind her—his father, General Richard Sterling, strapped to a chair at the conference table, his face bruised but his eyes defiant.

"Pops," Blake instinctively moved forward before Derek's iron grip restrained him.

"Wait," Derek whispered. "We need a plan. There are at least twelve armed operators in there."

Before they could formulate a strategy, the decision was made for them. The door swung fully open, revealing Sarah Foster with a pistol aimed directly at Blake's chest.

"Mr. Sterling," she said calmly, as if welcoming him to another podcast interview. "I'm so glad you could join us. Please, come in. Your father and I were just discussing the finer points of corporate responsibility."

Blake, Madison, and Derek found themselves quickly disarmed and marched into the conference room, where the tactical operators formed a perimeter around them. General Sterling's eyes widened at the sight of his son.

"Blake? What are you doing here? You were supposed to be safe in the analog district!"

"Safe?" Blake replied incredulously. "The entire Rage-Box network is hunting us! The cops are hunting us!"

Sarah Foster moved between them, her expression coldly satisfied. "Family reunion complete. How fitting that you're all here to witness the culmination of our work."

"Your work for Nexus, you mean," Derek spat, earning a surprised look from Sarah.

"You've done your homework, Mr. Santos. Yes, Nexus Defense Systems has been a generous supporter of our cause. They understand, as Sterling never did, that highway violence requires a systemic solution, not more weapons in untrained hands."

"They're using you," Madison spoke up, her ragefluencer voice now completely gone. "This isn't about safety—it's about market control."

Sarah's expression flickered briefly before hardening again. "That's a convenient lie, isn't it? Sterling has always tried to discredit our movement, whereas Nexus supported our advocacy after Erica died—when no one else would."

"They approached you because you were useful," Derek countered. "A grieving mother with a legitimate cause—the perfect front for corporate warfare. They never cared about you or Erica. They saw an opportunity to weaponize your grief."

Sarah's hand tightened around her pistol as she processed this information. But before she could respond, one of the tactical operatives approached, whispering something in her ear. Her expression cleared, resolve returning to her features.

"It doesn't matter now," she announced, checking her watch while handing her gun to one of the operatives. "Keep on eye on them. The demonstration begins in ten minutes. Nexus is going to get what they want. And I'll get what I want, too."

She moved to a weapons case on the conference table, opening it to reveal a state-of-the-art Sterling Defense assault rifle. With an ease that would have been unexpected from someone protesting violence, she checked the weapon and loaded a magazine.

"Your family's weapons killed my daughter Erica," she said, chambering a round as she turned toward Blake. "Time for some field testing of your latest product line."

The hollow click of the rifle's safety being disengaged echoed through the suddenly silent room as Blake, Madison, and Derek exchanged desperate glances, searching for any possible escape from what appeared to be the final consequence of a system they had helped create.

CHAPTER 7

GOING VIRAL AGAIN

Sarah Foster's finger hovered over the trigger of her Sterling Defense assault rifle, the barrel aimed directly at Blake's chest. The abandoned military base's conference room fell silent, except for the soft electronic hum of tactical equipment and the rapid breathing of those present.

"You took my child. Now I'm going to take yours," Sarah looked directly at General Sterling while keeping the rifle trained on Blake.

General Sterling tried to break out of his restraints, the chair creaking beneath him. "Ms. Foster, I understand your anger, but—"

"You understand nothing," Sarah snapped, momentarily shifting her aim to the older Sterling. "Your company designed a system that gamifies violence, that rewards aggression, that turns everyday drivers into killers. And your son..." She swung the rifle back toward Blake, "...your son and his fiancée made it all trendy."

"I'm sorry if you feel like we somehow contributed to your daughter's death," Madison said, her voice steady despite the gravity of the situation. "But this won't bring Erica back."

Sarah's eyes narrowed, but her aim remained steady. "No, it won't. But it will ensure no other parent has to experience what I did." She adjusted her grip on the weapon. "The Sterling family has profited from highway violence long enough. Your system turned road rage into entertainment, accidents into viral content, and my daughter's death into a quarterly earnings boost. And besides, you know what the Bible says... an eye for an eye."

Blake raised his hands slowly. "Sarah, please. We've learned—"

"Learned what?" Sarah's laugh was bitter and hollow. "That actions have consequences? Isn't that what you always said in your videos? Well, welcome to the consequences."

Madison glanced around the room, assessing their dire situation. Derek stood motionless beside them, his experienced eyes scanning for any possible advantage. Behind Sarah, at least a dozen Nexus operatives in tactical gear formed an impenetrable barrier. Through the windows, Madison could see more armed personnel establishing a perimeter around the building.

"You're being used," Derek said calmly. "Nexus doesn't care about highway safety. They care about eliminating their competition."

Sarah's jaw tightened. "They gave me a platform when no one else would listen. They funded our advocacy work when Sterling's lawyers were burying us in legal motions. They're helping me expose the truth."

"By executing us on camera?" Madison asked, nodding toward the livestreaming equipment positioned around the room. "How is that different from what you claim we did?"

A flicker of doubt crossed Sarah's face before she steeled herself again. "The difference is purpose. This isn't entertainment. This is justice."

One of the Nexus operatives approached, checking his watch. "We're live in three minutes, Ms. Foster. The stream is being routed through untraceable servers. Current viewer count is already at 1.7 million and climbing."

Sarah nodded. "Perfect. Help the General up. I want him front and center when we begin."

Two operatives moved to General Sterling, cutting his restraints but keeping their weapons trained on him as they roughly positioned him beside Blake and Madison.

"This is pointless. My security team will find us," General Sterling muttered. "Sterling Defense has protocols for executive extraction."

"Your security team has already been neutralized," Sarah replied coldly. "Your compound is under Nexus control. Your RageBox network has been compromised. Right now, the entire world is about to witness the fall of Sterling Defense—live and unfiltered."

Blake exchanged a desperate look with Madison. In that moment, without words, they shared a devastating realization: they had helped create this reality. Their content, their platform, their influence had normalized the very violence now threatening to end their lives.

Sarah turned to face the main camera. "Prepare for transmission. Let's show the world what happens when highway violence comes home to its creators."

Just as Sarah raised her hand to signal the broadcast start, a distant alarm began blaring. The concrete walls of the military base vibrated with the ancient warning system's wail.

"What the heck is that?" Sarah demanded, her concentration broken.

A Nexus operative rushed to the window. "Perimeter breach! Multiple vehicles approaching at high speed!"

"Our extraction team?" General Sterling asked, hope flickering in his eyes.

The operative's voice was tight with confusion. "No. They're... civilians. Dozens of them. Modified vehicles, heavily armed."

Sarah strode to the window, rifle still in hand. Through the darkness, a shocking sight greeted her: a convoy of wildly customized vehicles racing toward the base, their headlights cutting through the night like predatory eyes. Monster trucks with reinforced battering rams, SUVs bristling with improvised weapons, even converted school buses armored with scrap metal.

"What is happening right now?" Sarah whispered, genuine confusion replacing her cold confidence.

Derek checked his watch and a small, knowing smile crossed his face. "Right on time."

Blake moved cautiously to the window. His eyes widened as he recognized the lead vehicle—a massive pickup truck with "ROAD WARRIOR 452" emblazoned across its hood in flaming letters. Behind it, a suburban minivan painted with tiger stripes bore the unmistakable logo of "THE REAL HIGHWAY QUEEN."

"Babe," Blake breathed. "It's our followers."

Madison smiled. "Highway Nation. They've come to rescue us. How did you know they'd come to help?"

"Um, actually, I thought it was my guys, not yours," Derek he checked his watch again. "I knew your some of your fanbase had been organizing something through encrypted channels. I really thought it was a con or some sort of meetup, but I never expected this."

Outside, the ragtag convoy smashed through what was left of the outer gate, livestreaming their approach from dozens of angles. Homemade drones buzzed overhead, capturing the chaos as Nexus security personnel scrambled to respond.

Sarah's plan was unraveling before her eyes. "Lock down the building! No one gets in or out!"

But it was too late. The first explosions rocked the perimeter as Blake and Madison's most devoted fans deployed makeshift breaching charges against the facility's doors. Through the windows, they could see figures in homemade tactical gear—suburban dads, teenage gear-heads, soccer moms transformed into self-styled highway warriors—charging toward the building.

"This is insanity," Madison whispered, her voice cracking. "They're going to get themselves killed."

Derek nodded grimly. "That's the problem with creating a cult of personality around violence. Sometimes your followers decide to join the fight."

The main monitor in the conference room suddenly flickered to life, displaying multiple livestreams from the approaching vehicles. The comment sections were exploding with activity:

RoadWarrior452: HIGHWAY NATION ASSEMBLE!!! FREE BLAKE AND MADISON!!!TheReal-HighwayQueen: I brought my whole mom group!!! We are LOCKED AND LOADED!!BloodOnTheAsphalt: First time using my dad's guns IRL!!! So hyped rn!!!Sterling4Life: Death to Nexus traitors!!! Highway justice incoming!!!

Blake stared at the screens in horror. "They think this is some kind of game. They don't understand what they're walking into."

Another explosion, closer this time, shook the building. The Nexus operatives exchanged knowing glances as dust rained from the ceiling.

"Ms. Foster," one of them said calmly and sounding a bit patronizing, "some of these vehicles are displaying Nexus identification codes. They're our people, disguised as civilians."

Sarah's eyes widened. "What? That wasn't part of the plan."

"Protocol activated," the Nexus operative announced into his comm. "Operation Cleanup is now in effect. No witnesses, no evidence, no survivors."

Derek's expression darkened. "They're not just eliminating loose ends—they're destroying the entire operation. Everyone here is expendable now."

Madison grabbed Blake's arm. "They're going to massacre them—our followers, our fans. People who think they're helping us."

Blake felt sick. These were people who'd watched their content, who'd believed in their message, who'd internalized every word about "highway justice" and "consequences for violations." And now they were charging headlong into a slaughter, all while livestreaming it for likes and shares.

The first gunshots echoed through the building as Nexus operatives engaged with the intruders. They continued broadcasting, capturing every moment of the escalating chaos.

Sarah stood frozen, her carefully planned execution of the Sterlings forgotten as she watched events spiral beyond her control. "This isn't what I wanted," she murmured, almost to herself. "This was supposed to be controlled and precise—a statement against corporate violence, not... not this."

Derek moved with sudden, fluid precision, disarming the distracted Nexus operative nearest to him and securing the man's sidearm in one smooth motion. Before anyone could react, he had positioned himself between the Sterlings and the remaining operatives.

"Nobody moves," Derek commanded, his stance revealing years of professional training far beyond what any ragefluencer should possess. "Blake, Madison, General—behind me, now."

Blake blinked in shock at Derek's transformation. "Um, I thought you said you were a cybersecurity consultant? How does a cybersecurity dude move like some sort of Jack Bauer? I mean, who are you really?"

"Later," Derek replied tersely, eyes never leaving the Nexus operatives. "Right now, we need to contain this situation before more civilians get hurt."

Another explosion rocked the building, this one close enough to shatter the conference room windows. Through the broken glass, they could see the chaotic battle unfolding across the base grounds—Blake's followers engaged in firefights with Nexus security, both sides taking casualties, all while dozens of amateur livestreams captured the carnage.

Madison spotted a familiar figure charging toward the building—a suburban mother in makeshift body armor emblazoned with the Highway Nation logo, wielding what appeared to be her husband's hunting rifle. With horror, Madison recognized her as Jessica, one of their most dedicated commenters who called herself "TheRealHighwayQueen."

"They're going to die for us," Madison whispered, her voice breaking. "They think this is like our videos. They don't understand this is real."

As if confirming her fears, a teenage boy in tactical gear rushed past the window, shouting excitedly into his phone camera: "BloodOnTheAsphalt coming at you live! We're rescuing Blake and Madison! So if you're enjoying this livestream, don't forget to like and subscribe!"

Seconds later, gunfire erupted, and the teen's phone tumbled to the ground with the camera only capturing the sky now as he cried out in pain.

Blake felt something break inside him. "We have to stop this."

Sarah Foster stood paralyzed, the rifle hanging limply in her hands as she watched her revenge plan transform into something far more horrific. "This isn't justice," she murmured. "This is just... more death."

A Nexus operative near the door suddenly raised his weapon toward her. "Sorry, ma'am, they said no witnesses."

Derek's reaction was instantaneous. He fired once, dropping the operative before the man could squeeze his trigger. Sarah stumbled backward in shock as Derek positioned himself protectively in front of her as well.

"They're eliminating loose ends," Derek explained grimly. "Including you, Ms. Foster. You've served your purpose."

Understanding dawned in Sarah's eyes—the horrible realization that she had been manipulated, her grief weaponized for corporate warfare. "They needed Sterling to look like the problem," she murmured. "So they could sell themselves as the solution."

"Nexus Guardian Systems," Derek confirmed. "Fully autonomous, no human control, complete surveillance. They just needed to eliminate the competition first. And all of this greed led to your daughter's death."

"You mean—" Sarah couldn't find a way to say the rest. The realization that she was not only a pawn for taking down Sterling Defense but also assisting the people who killed her daughter left her speechless.

Derek found the words Sarah couldn't. "Yes, Nexus our daughter away from you."

building shook again as more of Blake and Madi-
lowers breached the main entrance. Through the
ce room's open door, they could hear the chaos

approaching—shouted catchphrases from Highway Nation videos, amateur tactical commands, the terrifying enthusiasm of people who thought they were participating in content rather than combat.

Madison's gaze fixed on a tactical equipment case in the corner. With sudden determination, she broke from Derek's protection and lunged for it, extracting what she needed—a megaphone.

"Madison!" Blake called out in alarm.

"We started this," she replied, her voice steady with newfound resolve. "And we need to end it."

Outside, the battle raged on across multiple fronts. Nexus operatives in civilian disguise had begun firing on Blake and Madison's real followers, creating a three-way conflict that was spiraling further out of control with each passing minute. The livestreams continued unabated, with millions now watching the carnage unfold in real-time.

The most devoted fans had reached the building's main entrance, led by Marcus, the veteran behind the "Road-Warrior452" account. "HIGHWAY NATION!" he bellowed, raising a Sterling Defense tactical shotgun above his head. "LET'S FREE OUR HEROES!"

Madison positioned herself at the shattered window, megaphone in hand. For a moment, she froze—the weigh of responsibility crushing down on her. Then she raised it to her lips.

"HIGHWAY NATION, STOP!" Her amplified voice cut through the chaos like a physical force. "THIS ENDS NOW!"

The effect was immediate but incomplete. Some fighters paused, recognizing the voice of their idol. Others continued the battle, too caught up in the adrenaline rush to process the command.

Blake moved to Madison's side, taking the megaphone from her hands. "EVERYONE STOP FIGHTING! GO HOME! WE'RE NOT WORTH DYING FOR!"

Marcus looked up in confusion, his weapon lowering slightly. "But... we came to save you! Highway justice demands—"

"THERE IS NO HIGHWAY JUSTICE!" Blake roared into the megaphone, his voice cracking with emotion. "WE WERE USED! ALL OF IT WAS A LIE TO MAKE MONEY!"

A murmur of confusion spread through the ranks of his followers. Some began to back away, the reality of the situation finally penetrating the fantasy they'd constructed.

Others, however, became enraged. "TRAITORS!" someone shouted from the crowd. "THEY'VE BEEN TURNED AGAINST US!"

The situation teetered on the edge of chaos. Meanwhile, the Nexus operatives were regrouping to get their Plan B, AKA eliminate all witnesses, moving outside.

Inside, Sarah Foster made her decision. She stepped forward, taking the megaphone from Blake. "MY NAME IS SARAH FOSTER," she announced, her voice carrying across the battlefield. "NEXUS DEFENSE SYSTEMS USED ME TO CREATE THIS CONFLICT! THEY MANIPULATED MY GRIEF OVER MY DAUGHTER'S DEATH TO SERVE THEIR CORPORATE AGENDA! THEY'RE NOW ATTEMPTING TO ELIMINATE ME AND ALL OF YOU!"

She paused, emotion threatening to overcome her. "I wanted justice for Erica. Instead, I almost became what killed her. Don't make the same mistake I did. THIS ISN'T A GAME OR A LIVESTREAM! THIS IS REAL, AND PEOPLE ARE DYING!"

Her words reached some of the fighters, who began to lower their weapons and back away from the conflict. But the Nexus operatives had no intention of allowing witnesses to escape, and they opened fire on retreating civilians, creating renewed panic.

Derek moved with practiced efficiency, herding the Sterlings, Madison, and Sarah toward a side exit. "We need to move now. This situation is beyond containment."

As they navigated through the chaos, Blake witnessed the horror their content had created—ordinary people transformed into warriors, armed with Sterling Defense products, fighting and dying for their parasocial relationship, the connection they believed they had with him and Madison.

A Nexus operative appeared in their path, weapon raised. Before Derek could react, a shot rang out—from Sarah's rifle. The operative crumpled to the ground as Sarah lowered the smoking barrel.

"They used my daughter," she said simply, her eyes hard with newfound clarity.

They reached a service corridor leading toward the rear of the facility. Through windows along the passage, they could see the battle continuing to rage across the compound grounds. News helicopters had arrived, their spotlights sweeping the scene as they broadcast the conflict to an even wider audience.

"The entire world is watching this," Madison realized aloud. "Highway justice isn't just entertainment anymore. It's a nightmare playing out on every screen."

They burst through an emergency exit into the cool night air, only to find themselves face-to-face with more Nexus operatives establishing a perimeter. Before the enemy could react, precise shots rang out from the darkness, dropping the operatives where they stood.'

Derek nodded toward shadowy figures moving efficiently through the compound. "Contractors hired by Sterling Defense for extraction scenarios. Your father's been planning for this possibility since the Nexus investigation began."

"How long has this operation been running?" Blake demanded.

"Eighteen months. Since I first made contact with Nexus recruiters through the ragefluencer network."

Before Blake could respond, more of Derek's team arrived, securing a perimeter around them. One agent approached with a medical kit, immediately attending to General Sterling's injuries.

"Extraction vehicles are two minutes out, sir," the agent reported to Derek. "We're beginning to neutralize Nexus operations."

"And the civilians?" Madison asked, her voice tight with concern.

The agent's expression was grim. "Local law enforcement is responding, but casualties are... significant." He took in a deep breath and shook his head from side to side before continuing. "Many of them are still livestreaming, refusing to retreat even under fire."

Blake felt physically ill. These were people who had watched his content, who had internalized his message that highway violence was just "educational" entertainment with no real consequences. Now they were dying while trying to capture the perfect angle for their followers.

A series of explosions rocked the main building as Nexus operatives began destroying evidence. The fires spread quickly, illuminating the battlefield in flickering orange light. Through the chaos, Derek's team led them to armored vehicles waiting at the compound's rear entrance.

As they prepared to evacuate, Blake turned to see Sarah Foster standing apart from the group, watching the destruction with tears streaming down her face.

"Sarah," he called out. "Come with us. Help us expose what really happened."

She shook her head slowly. "I need to stay. There are wounded out there—people who came because they believed in something. I can't abandon them to die for a lie."

Before Blake could argue with her, Derek placed a hand on his shoulder. "It's okay. My team will protect her."

As their vehicle pulled away from the burning compound, Blake and Madison watched through the bulletproof windows as the battle continued to rage. News helicopters circled overhead, broadcasting the unprecedented three-way conflict between Nexus operatives, Highway Nation loyalists, and law enforcement to a global audience.

"How many will die tonight because of us?" Madison whispered, her perfect ragefluencer mask completely shattered, eyes welling up with tears.

Blake had no answer. He simply took her hand, both of them watching in silent horror as the system they had promoted imploded spectacularly on worldwide media.

In the front seat, Derek checked a secure device that had just chimed with an incoming message. His expression remained unreadable as he processed the information.

"What is it?" General Sterling demanded.

Derek tucked the device away before responding. "Phase Two initiated."

Blake leaned forward, suspicion rekindling in his eyes. "How much of this was real? Any of it?"

Derek's gaze met his in the rearview mirror. "Your growth was real. Your choices were real. Everything else was just theater."

Madison's fingers tightened around Blake's as a terrible realization dawned on her. "We're not the main characters in this story, are we?"

Derek didn't answer. He didn't need to. Behind them, the abandoned military base burned against the night sky, its flames reflected in millions of screens worldwide as the livestreamed battle changed public perception of highway violence forever.

The rage had gone viral one final time.

CHAPTER 8

NEW ALGORITHM

The six months since the military base incident had been a blur of congressional hearings, media interviews, and legal proceedings. Blake and Madison had testified before three separate committees, their former content dissected frame by frame as evidence of the system's manipulation.

Their transformation hadn't been clean or simple. Blake still woke up some mornings reaching for his phone to check engagement metrics that no longer mattered. Madison caught herself planning content before remembering that wasn't the point anymore.

Blake sat in one of the most basic-of-basic sedans out in front of a storefront that read "Sterling Safe Driving Academy" in simple black letters. No flashy logo, no catchy slogan about conquering the road or dominating traffic—just a straightforward promise of safety. The small East Hollywood establishment occupied what had once been a laundromat, its large windows now decorated with hand-painted reminders about proper following distance and blind spot awareness.

Blake adjusted the sedan's rearview mirror. Gone was the vehicle that had reinforced bumpers, tactical defense systems, or any of the military-grade upgrades he once showcased to millions of followers. It didn't even have a RageBox.

"Remember, Maria," Blake said to the nervous six-teen-year-old behind the wheel, "mirrors, signal, then change lanes—in that order. And always maintain a safe following distance."

Maria nodded as she held the steering wheel. "But what if someone cuts me off? Don't I need to, like, you know, establish dominance or something?"

Blake smiled patiently. "No one needs to establish dom-inance on the road. That's what got us into this mess in the first place." He gestured toward the street outside. "Your job is to get where you're going safely—not to teach anyone a lesson."

Six months ago, Blake would have been filming this interaction, positioning cameras for optimal engagement while suggesting aggressive maneuvers that would gener-ate more views. Now, there were no cameras, no performance, no content strategy—just an ex-ragefluencer trying to undo some of the damage he'd caused.

"My brother says the analog district is for losers who can't afford RageBox systems," Maria confessed as she cautiously pulled into traffic. "He says real driving happens in the Rage Lanes."

Blake watched as she signaled properly before changing lanes, her movements deliberate and measured. "Your brother's been watching too many ragefluencer videos. Real driving is cooperation, not a competition. It's about getting *everyone* home safely."

As they drove through the analog district, Blake observed other student drivers practicing in unmodified vehicles. These teenagers had made a conscious choice to learn in the analog zone—rejecting the RageBox dependency that had become the norm for their generation. Many had watched the livestreamed battle at the Citizens Against Highway Violence compound six months ago, witnessing firsthand how the performative violence Blake once championed had led to real bloodshed.

"But come on.... don't you, like, miss it?" Maria asked suddenly. "It must've been so awesome being famous. I mean, you, like, had millions of followers and all those cool tactical vehicles?"

Blake considered the question as he watched her navigate the intersection safely—no aggressive moves, no content opportunities, just competent driving. "I thought I would," he admitted. "But teaching you and others like you how to drive gives me way more satisfaction than any viral video ever did."

"Really?"

"Yes, really."

It was true, though the adjustment hadn't been easy. Some days he still felt the phantom buzz of notifications that would never come again.

The realization still surprised him sometimes—how genuine fulfillment felt different from the dopamine hits of social media. He watched Maria navigate a four-way stop with the appropriate amount of caution, yielding to other drivers rather than asserting priority. The pride he felt in that outweighed any engagement statistic he'd ever achieved.

Ten miles away, in a converted warehouse that housed "Peace in Motion FM," Madison Perdew adjusted her headphones and leaned toward the microphone. The analog radio station's equipment was decades old—functional, but far from the state-of-the-art streaming setup she'd once commanded.

"Good afternoon, East Hollywood. This is Madison with your traffic report." Her voice carried none of the fake excitement or manufactured outrage that had once been her trademark. Instead, she spoke with calm clarity. "We've got congestion on Sunset between Vermont and Western. Remember to leave early and plan your route to avoid frustration. And remember, patience is always faster than aggression."

The station's calls lit up immediately.

"Caller, you're on the air with Peace in Motion," Madison said, pressing the button for Line 1.

"Hi, Madison. There's construction on Los Feliz causing some backups. But the workers have set up really clear detour signs."

"Thanks for that information," Madison replied. "Everyone hear that? Clear signage, just follow the detours, and remember, slow for the cone zone. Those workers have families, too. And they want to get home to them, just like you. So no need for frustration—the road crews are just doing their jobs."

As Madison continued taking calls, she glanced at the small cluster of photographs taped to her console—images of traffic accident victims whose stories she had once exploited for content. Now, their memories served as a daily reminder of why her work mattered.

The station's primary audience consisted of analog district residents who had rejected RageBox technology, along with people from outside the district trying to recover from what doctors were now calling "rage dependency syndrome." For many, Madison's voice had become an anchor in their recovery—the same voice that had once encouraged their worst impulses was now guiding them toward cooperation.

"Remember, East Hollywood," Madison said as her segment neared its end, "every car contains a human being with loved ones waiting for them to arrive safely. When we remember that simple fact, traffic becomes a community effort rather than a competition."

She switched off her microphone and sat back, allowing herself a moment of quiet satisfaction. Six months ago, she had measured her worth in sponsored content deals and engagement analytics. Now, she found meaning in the simple act of helping people navigate their day without violence.

Her producer poked his head into the studio. "Great show today."

Madison nodded, no longer feeling the compulsive need to check metrics or compare performance to competitors. "Thanks. But honestly, I'm just happy people are finding it useful."

The realization still caught her by surprise some-times—that she genuinely enjoyed helping people solve problems rather than exploiting their worst instincts for views.

Across town, in a modest office space adorned with photographs of highways reimagined as community spaces, Sarah Foster led a meeting of her new organiza-tion, "Citizens for Highway Healing." Sarah's organiza-tion faced constant legal challenges from both Sterling and Nexus. Corporate accountability was messier in reality than in their idealistic plans. The congressional hearings had generated headlines but little concrete change.

But the work continued—one intersection redesign, one driver education program, one reformed ragefluencer at a time. The highway violence epidemic wasn't solved, but somewhere in East Hollywood, teenagers learned to drive without weapons systems, and for the first time in years, that felt like progress.

The conference table was surrounded by urban plan-ners, trauma counselors, and former road rage victims—a coalition united by the shared goal of transforming Amer-ica's driving culture.

"The infrastructure proposal goes before the city coun-cil next week," Sarah explained, gesturing to the blueprints spread across the table. "If approved, it would replace three Rage Lanes with HOV lanes and dedicated bus corridors."

"Will Sterling Defense oppose it?" asked a community organizer, the concern evident in his voice.

Sarah shook her head. "Actually, their new leadership has agreed to remain neutral. It's a small victory, but significant."

The transformation in Sarah was profound. Six months ago, she had been a grieving mother manipulated into seeking vengeance. Now, she channeled her pain into systematic change—lobbying for better road design, comprehensive driver education, and mental health support for road rage victims.

Twice weekly, she attended therapy sessions to process both her daughter Erica's death and her own manipulation by Nexus. The journey was a little bumpy—some days the grief and guilt threatened to overwhelm her—but she remained committed to creating meaning from tragedy.

As the meeting concluded, Sarah noticed Blake and Madison waiting outside her office. Their relationship had evolved from adversaries to cautious allies, united by the shared experience of being used as pawns in a larger game. The three nodded to each other—a simple acknowledgment that contained volumes of unspoken understanding.

"Blake, Madison," Sarah greeted them with reserved warmth. "I wasn't expecting you today."

"We saw your proposal for the Highway Healing Center," Blake said. "We'd like to help, you know, if you'll have us."

Sarah studied them carefully. Six months ago, such an offer would have seemed like a cynical publicity stunt. Now, she recognized the genuine commitment in their eyes—the same hard-earned wisdom she saw in her own mirror each morning.

"Come in," she said finally. "We could use your perspective."

While Blake, Madison, and Sarah worked to rebuild from the ground up, the corporate war continued to play out with Sterling Defense and Nexus engaged in battles far removed from the streets where their products were deployed.

General Richard Sterling, his bearing unchanged despite the events of the past six months, testified before a congressional committee investigating highway violence and corporate responsibility.

"The RageBox system was designed with safeguards that were systematically undermined," he stated, his voice carrying the weight of reluctant admission. "Nexus Defense exploited vulnerabilities we should have anticipated. For that failure, Sterling Defense accepts responsibility."

On screens throughout the hearing room, footage from the livestreamed battle played on loop—ordinary citizens wielding Sterling and Nexus products against each other while corporate operatives manipulated the conflict from behind the scenes. The images had become iconic, reshaping public perception of the highway violence epidemic that both companies had profited from.

Nexus executives occupied the witness table the following day, offering carefully crafted statements about "industry-wide challenges" and "shared responsibility." Like so many companies before them, they had their patsies, blaming the whole ordeal on rogue employees. With their sacrificial lambs facing criminal prosecution for their role in weaponizing Sarah Foster's grief, the company now operated under new leadership that promised reform while delivering more of the same.

Despite the corporate failure to take real accountability and evolve, there was a cultural shift taking root. Not in the corporate world or with the politicians, but at least the younger generation seemed to have taken note of what happened. Blake, Madison, and Sarah would continue to use their fame as they fought to make a positive change in their communities, and hopefully, the world.

***

Books often struggle to get noticed. If you enjoyed this book, please consider leaving a review. Thank you!

GET A FREE BOOK!

Join my newsletter and get a FREE BOOK!

BONUS CHAPTER

RECRUITMENT

Three years before the confrontation

The private dining room at Caterina's exuded historic Washington power—wood paneling harvested from extinct forests, oil paintings of forgotten statesmen, and lighting calibrated to make everyone look slightly more trustworthy than they actually were. Derek Santos adjusted his collar, his reflection revealing a man perfectly assembled on the outside—tailored suit, precision haircut, shoes that conveyed both success and restraint. Yet his eyes betrayed his carefully construction of normalcy—hollow, unfocused, occasionally drifting somewhere else altogether.

Six months. One hundred and eighty-three days since the accident. Four thousand three hundred and ninety-two hours of going through the motions...

The maître d' appeared at his elbow. "General Sterling has arrived, Mr. Santos."

Derek nodded, straightening papers that needed no straightening. Santos Cybersecurity had received the meeting request through official channels—a Sterling Defense consultation on "confidential security matters." Standard corporate work that paid well and required minimal emotional investment. Exactly what Derek needed to keep functioning.

General Richard Sterling entered, his posture and stride sharing more about his background than the impeccably tailored suit ever could. He moved with the confidence of a man accustomed to others following his commands.

"Mr. Santos." Sterling extended his hand. "Thank you for making time."

"Of course, General. My team has prepared some preliminary assessments of your network vulnerabilities." Derek gestured to the leather portfolio on the table. "Though typically we'd start with a more comprehensive—"

"I didn't come to discuss your standard corporate package." Sterling sat down in the chair across from Derek, studying him with unsettling intensity. "I understand you lost your daughter six months ago."

Derek's professional smile froze, the sudden intrusion of reality into the carefully constructed fiction of normal business cracking his composure. "That's not why you called this meeting."

"Actually, it is." Sterling's voice remained level, his eyes never leaving Derek's face. "Emilia Santos, eight years old, killed in a highway incident."

The name hit Derek like a physical blow. He flinched visibly, his fingers tightening around the stem of his water glass as he fought to maintain his professional mask. Nobody said her name anymore. Everyone in his life had learned to navigate around it, to use euphemisms—"your loss," "the accident," "what happened"—never "Emilia."

"How do you—" Derek started, then recalibrated. "My personal life isn't relevant to Sterling Defense's security needs."

"It's entirely relevant to what I'm about to propose." Sterling placed his napkin in his lap. "The incident report stated you blamed yourself. That you believed your attempt to de-escalate the situation actually made it worse."

Derek's composure began to fracture further. Those weren't public details. He'd never shared that with anyone except the responding officer, and even then, only in the shock of the moment, before he built a wall around his emotions.

"I should have been more careful," Derek admitted, the words escaping before he could stop them. "Should have seen the aggression earlier."

The memory surfaced with brutal clarity—a routine morning, driving Emilia to school, her voice in the back seat practicing multiplication tables. The black SUV appearing in his rearview mirror, following too closely. Derek changing lanes to let them pass. The SUV changing lanes, matching him, engine revving aggressively.

"I tried to de-escalate," Derek continued, his voice hollow. "Slowed down, changed lanes again, gave them plenty of room. I thought I was being responsible."

Sterling nodded, his expression revealing nothing. "And then?"

"The driver interpreted it as weakness." Derek's voice hardened. "Escalated the confrontation. Tried to force us off the road. When I wouldn't yield completely, he..."

The words stuck in his throat. The crash. The impact. The silence afterward, more terrible than any sound he'd ever heard.

"If I'd just driven normally, hadn't tried to avoid conflict, she'd still be alive."

Sterling waited a beat, allowing the raw confession to settle between them before responding. "Sterling Defense conducted a private analysis of your daughter's accident."

"Why would your company investigate a random traffic death?" Derek's professional suspicion broke through his grief, sharpening his focus.

"Because it wasn't random." Sterling reached into his briefcase, extracting a slim folder. "The other driver was using modified Sterling Defense equipment."

He slid photographs and other documents across the table—high-resolution images of twisted metal, technical diagrams annotated with measurement data, financial records, and transaction logs.

Derek's confusion deepened as he scanned the documents. "Your equipment failed?"

"The equipment was counterfeit." Sterling's voice hardened. "Manufactured by Nexus Defense."

The name registered dimly in Derek's mind—Sterling's primary competitor in the civilian defense market.

"Nexus has been flooding the market with defective Sterling knockoffs," Sterling continued, pointing to technical specifications. "The targeting systems are deliberately miscalibrated. The threat assessment algorithms are compromised. The safety protocols are disabled."

Derek studied the documents with growing horror. "Why would they do this?"

"To create failures that discredit Sterling products while positioning Nexus as the 'safer' alternative." Sterling's jaw tightened almost imperceptibly.

The implications assembled themselves in Derek's mind with sickening clarity. "Wait. You're saying my daughter died because some corporation wanted to make more money?"

"Nexus is deliberately causing casualties to steal market share." Sterling confirmed, his corporate jargon unable to fully sanitize the atrocity he was describing.

Derek stared at the documents, professional detachment warring with parental anguish. "How many?"

Sterling opened another folder, revealing data visualizations tracking dozens of similar incidents across multiple states. Pattern analyses. Demographic profiles. Casualty statistics coded in clinical blues and reds.

"They've perfected the methodology," Sterling explained. "Identify aggressive drivers through their social media activity. Sell them knockoff Sterling systems at a huge discounted rate through shell distributors. When the systems inevitably fail and cause casualties, Nexus-funded 'safety advocates' emerge to blame Sterling for the resulting deaths."

"How many people have died for their business plan?" Derek's voice had gone dangerously quiet.

Sterling met his gaze directly. "Conservative estimate? Over two hundred in the past year."

The room seemed to contract around Derek as the number registered. Not just Emilia. Hundreds like her. Hundreds of families destroyed by corporate warfare disguised as traffic accidents.

"Why tell me this?" Derek asked finally, though he already suspected the answer.

"Because you understand both cybersecurity and the psychology of online radicalization." Sterling leaned forward slightly. "Your academic background in behavioral psychology combined with your practical experience tracking extremist recruitment patterns. Throw in your military background, and you have exactly the talents for what we need."

"Which is what, exactly?"

"Infiltration of ragefluencer networks to document Nexus's influence operations. We need evidence of their direct involvement in distributing faulty equipment and manipulating public perception."

Derek laughed at the thought. "Um, I'm not a spy. I'm a cybersecurity consultant."

"You're a father who understands what Nexus steals from families." Sterling's voice remained steady. "They weaponized your grief the same way they'll weaponize others. The same psychology that makes you blame your-self for trying to de-escalate—that's what they exploit."

The professional part of Derek's mind recognized the manipulation in Sterling's approach, the calculated appeal to his emotions. Yet he couldn't deny his interest in the technical challenge. The complexity of the counterintel-ligence operation. The opportunity to understand how Nexus had identified and targeted the driver who killed Emilia.

"I'd need access to your intelligence on Nexus op-erations," Derek said, allowing himself to consider the proposition professionally.

"Full access," Sterling agreed immediately. "Everything we have."

"Everything?" Derek's voice hardened. "Every file, every analysis, every victim profile? Nothing held back?"

"Everything we have," Sterling repeated. "Plus Depart-ment of Transportation classification access."

A silence settled between them as Derek processed the offer. Sterling reached down beside his chair and lifted a metal briefcase onto the table. He entered a combination, the locks disengaging with precise mechanical clicks.

Inside, neatly stacked bundles of cash—more money than Derek had seen outside of movies.

"Five million in operational funding to start," Sterling stated matter-of-factly. "You'll need to build a credible ragefluencer persona, acquire equipment, establish networks."

Derek stared at the money. "This is a lot of money for a consulting contract."

"This isn't consulting." Sterling's gaze never wavered. "This is justice for Emilia and hundreds like her."

The unspoken truth hung in the air between them: it was also protection for Sterling Defense's market position. Corporate warfare fought through a grieving father.

Derek tried to evaluate the proposition dispassionately as a business arrangement. But the professional detachment he'd cultivated couldn't withstand the emotional undertow—the promise of understanding Emilia's death, of preventing others.

"How long would this operation take?" he asked, practical concerns asserting themselves.

"Could be months, could be years." Sterling's honesty was oddly reassuring. "Nexus is sophisticated. Their influence networks are deeply embedded."

"I've never done anything like this." Fear edged into Derek's voice—not of physical danger, but of the psychological toll of becoming something he was not.

Sterling outlined the technical details with military precision. Derek would become a ragefluencer. The goal was to get noticed by Nexus recruiters, to document their methods and collect evidence of the conspiracy. The DOT would provide backup identity and extraction protocols. Communication would be minimal—dead drops, encrypted channels only.

As Sterling spoke, Derek found himself staring at the only personal item he carried—a worn photograph of Emilia that he'd taken the week before she died. Her smile, captured forever at eight years old, a future that would never arrive.

"If I do this," Derek said finally, looking up from the photograph, "will you guarantee Nexus faces consequences?"

"Every executive involved in Emilia's death will face federal charges." Sterling's promise carried the weight of certainty, though whether from justice or corporate vengeance, Derek couldn't tell.

The weight of the decision pressed down on him. Professional ethics argued against becoming an operative in corporate warfare. Parental instinct demanded action against those responsible for Emilia's death. The two imperatives, irreconcilable in any rational framework, found alignment only in the distorted gravity of grief.